4/14

P9-DFT-761

THE GREAT AMERICAN WHATEVER

Also by Tim Federle

Better Nate Than Ever
Five, Six, Seven, Nate!

THE GREAT AMERICAN WHATEVER

TIM FEDERLE

SIMON & SCHUSTER BFYR

NEW YORK   LONDON   TORONTO   SYDNEY   NEW DELHI

SIMON & SCHUSTER BFYR

An imprint of Simon & Schuster Children's Publishing Division
1230 Avenue of the Americas, New York, New York 10020

SIMON & SCHUSTER BFYR is a trademark of Simon & Schuster, Inc.
For information about special discounts for bulk purchases, please contact Simon & Schuster Special Sales at 1-866-506-1949 or business@simonandschuster.com.
The Simon & Schuster Speakers Bureau can bring authors to your live event. For more information or to book an event, contact the Simon & Schuster Speakers Bureau at 1-866-248-3049 or visit our website at www.simonspeakers.com.
Jacket design by Krista Vossen
Interior design by Hilary Zarycky
The text for this book was set in Adobe Garamond Pro.
Manufactured in the United States of America
First Edition
2 4 6 8 10 9 7 5 3 1
Library of Congress Cataloging-in-Publication Data
Federle, Tim.
The great American whatever / Tim Federle.
pages cm
Summary: "Teenaged Quinn, an aspiring screenwriter, copes with his sister's death while his best friend forces him back out into the world to face his reality"— Provided by publisher.
ISBN 978-1-4814-0409-9 (hardback) — ISBN 978-1-4814-0411-2 (eBook)
[1. Screenwriters—Fiction. 2. Grief—Fiction. 3. Gays—Fiction.] I. Title.
PZ7.F314Gr 2016
[Fic]—dc23
2015015712

For *Ellie Batz*, who was impossible to forget,
and *Cheri Steinkellner*, who was impossible to ignore

THE GREAT AMERICAN WHATEVER

CHAPTER ONE

I don't consider myself to be precious, necessarily, but give me air-conditioning or give me death.

Maybe the only thing worse than a midwestern winter is a midwestern summer, especially when your AC is broken. We are going on our second straight week of record-breaking highs here. This is the universe's way of showing it has a sense of humor, since I am personally going on my sixth straight month of record-breaking lows.

"I have *got* to get a new air conditioner."

I actually say this out loud, just to hear a voice. Anyone's voice, really, these days.

"I have seriously *got*," I say again, crawling to the side of the bed and tricking my body into standing upright, "to get a new air conditioner." And then, a little louder: "I am requesting a new air conditioner from the universe."

Like if I say it enough times, the air-conditioning fairy will arrive. (Hey, you never know.) I give it twenty seconds. Alas, no fairy. Other than, you know, me.

I dare my feet to walk me to the bathroom so I can take a whiz, and then I lope back out to my bedroom, and all of this cardio makes me hot enough to formally debate "cooling-off options" that don't involve leaving my room.

I'd remove my clothes, but I'm already wearing only my lucky boxers, and every time I take them off these days, I'm like: *What's so wrong with me that I'm almost a senior and I still haven't been naked with another person?*

Great. See? And now I'm even hotter.

I keep my boxers on and move to the next option.

The mini-fridge that Mom got me two birthdays ago isn't quite big enough for me to comfortably lay my head inside—believe me, I've tried—and if I took out my broken AC and cracked the window, I'd have to confront the reality that I might hear, like, *birds*, or worse: the merry squeals of neighborhood children. And who has the stomach for that kind of unannounced joy at this hour?

So I go low-tech, slumping into my beanbag chair and fanning myself with a take-out menu. That's when some sweat rivulets drip from my elbow onto the floor, and not just that—that wouldn't be so bad—but my sweat hits a random page of an application for this lame student filmmakers' competition. Apparently I never got around to completing the application last fall, let alone sending it in. I can't seem to finish anything these days, except, oh, dessert.

I kick the form under my desk and decide to sneak downstairs and just stick my face in the freezer for a minute. Hey—maybe it'll shrink my pores at the same time. The school counselor calls that kind of thing multitasking, which she also claims is a dangerous myth. No, really. This is an actual, hand-to-God quote: *"Multitasking is a dangerous myth, Mr. Roberts."*

She always calls me "Mr. Roberts," probably as mildly embarrassed to say my first name as I am. Can't blame her there.

"Studies show that humans are able to pay attention to only one thing at a time, Mr. Roberts—are you listening to me?—and I'd prefer for you to pay more attention to your schoolwork than to your movies."

But the counselor was dead wrong, because as she was yammering on that day about how there's no such thing as multitasking, I was nodding *and* making earnest faces *and* imagining how incredible it would be if the school was hit by a freak comet. I was, you know, multitasking.

Obviously this was all before I stopped attending classes altogether.

Mom is downstairs on the wicker couch in our sunroom, snoozing as always. I tiptoe by and open the freezer, hoping some Popsicles will have magically appeared (the Popsicle fairy?), only to find a buttload of Healthy Choice meals.

OPEN QUESTION: Is it still a healthy choice if you have three of them in one sitting? Because that's how many are scattered around Mom's feet right now. She's really let herself go. See, Mom sort of eats her feelings—and this year has been nonstop feelings. The difference between us is that I can basically demolish a large pizza in under fifteen minutes and actually *lose* a few pounds, if I'm also worrying about my future while chewing.

I walk past a landfill's worth of unopened mail on our kitchen counter, with this hair salon postcard advertising "1/2 off BOLD new summer looks" sitting on top. "Maybe I'll trim my own hair today," I mumble to myself, careful not to wake Mom.

She's actually really cute when she's asleep.

Anyway, I could use a "BOLD new summer look," or an anything new summer anything. I've had the same haircut since I was a toddler—a style you might call "longish and brown." So maybe I'll finally do something different with it. To spice up the day. I don't know. My therapist has encouraged me "toward optimism."

I shut the freezer and trudge back upstairs to root around for a beard trimmer on Dad's shelf in the medicine cabinet. When he left, he just *left*. Meaning: All his stuff is still here. If you know anyone in the market for pleated knee-length shorts, let me know ASAP.

UPDATE: I'm back in my bathroom with Dad's rusty old

trimmer. It buzzes right on, and I consider it a minor financial triumph that at least the electricity hasn't been turned off around here. Maybe the local energy company has made it an unofficial policy not to screw with my mom for a few months. Our little community has basically written us an ongoing blank check of worried looks and faux concern—which is what happens when your big sister gets killed in a car wreck right outside the school on the day before Christmas break.

Oh. Spoiler alert.

So I'm lifting Dad's clippers to my sideburns—or attempting to, anyway—but I lose control of them, alarmed by a *thud* at my bedroom door. Jesus, I barely even heard Mom come up the stairs. Rare.

Thud. Thud. Thud.

Now the knocking is twice as loud, and not only because I've taken my earplugs out. (I've been wearing earplugs for a while now. They give the world a comforting dullness.)

"Mom, come *on*. You know this is 'me time.'"

It's been "me time" for about half a year now.

"It's not your mother," says my not-mother. "It's your Geoff."

Great. It was bound to happen. Old friends have a way of creeping up on you.

"I'm coming in."

"I'm naked," I lie.

"I don't care, Quinn."

Oh, it's Quinn, by the way. My name. What I'd give to be a John or a Mike or even an Evan. To be an Evan is to have been guaranteed a completely tragedy-free life, right from the get-go. What kind of dad names his first and only son Quinn?

(The kind who walks out without taking his pleated knee-length shorts or rusty clippers with him, that's the kind.)

Geoff kicks my door open. A *liiiittle* dramatic. My lock hasn't worked in, oh, forever.

"Dude," he says, grabbing his nose and laughing through his hand. Evidently it smells like I haven't had a shower in a month-ish, which I haven't-ish. "Your room makes *me* embarrassed to be a teenage boy," Geoff says, stepping inside. "And that's saying something, because I literally name my *farts*, for Pete's sake."

Poor Pete. Who is Pete? And why do people do such terrible things, just for his sake?

"Hey."

"Hey," Geoff says. "What happened to your *head*?"

I look back at the bathroom floor. A severe clump of my hair is lying in a heap by the sink, like it was making a prison break from my scalp and got gunned down. (If you haven't seen *Escape from Alcatraz*, by the way, put it on the list. Great movie.)

Anyway: "You startled me," I say to Geoff, "right in the middle of a thrilling autobiographical haircut."

But I'm not really pissed. In fact, the part of my head that's now missing the clump is feeling a little cooler, maybe. My first accomplishment in weeks. Heck, months.

"It's a good thing you're not ugly," Geoff says, and then: "It's actually kind of a not terrible look for you," he adds, squinting at me like it'll help shrink his exaggeration.

"I wasn't really asking for reviews," I say. "But thanks."

It's a bit of an insult to get judged by Geoff on my "look," as it were. I don't have a particularly adventurous sense of fashion, myself—give me jeans and a T-shirt and let's call it a day—but Geoff's outfits never even *fit* right. His clothes appear to be actively leaping from his body at all times, as if they're afraid to be seen in public with him. Today he's in a Steelers T-shirt, a pair of vaguely tragic camouflage cargo shorts, and neon-yellow flip-flops. Not to mention, bless him, an attempt at a mustache. This is new. Or new to me. It's been a while.

"We've got to get you out of the house, dude," he says. "Like to a movie or an Eat'n Park or something. Anything. *It's time.*"

My pulse thumps. I have to pull it together and start locking our front door. Food delivery guys just let themselves in these days and head straight up to my room. And now this.

I'm not ready for this.

"No way," I say. "It's a weekend. I don't want to run into anyone from school out there." I start waving my hands at the general direction of the window, like there's a zombie apocalypse happening on my block. A zombie apocalypse and not just, you know, Western Pennsylvania.

"It's *Wednesday*," Geoff says, laughing. "And it's the summer. So everybody's probably at the pool. You can duck down when we drive by."

It actually sounds amazing to dive into the pool right now. A freezing one. Headfirst. In the shallow end.

"*Dude*," Geoff says, noticing a stack of pizza boxes in the corner of the room that have, in my opinion, begun to take on an artistic still-life quality. "We're throwing those away. Today." But then he just looks at me and goes, "So?" Like I invited him over, which I did not! "What's the game plan?"

Accidentally, I speak: "Well, I kind of need to get a new air conditioner."

Geoff wipes his arm across his forehead. "Gee, you *think*?"

He crosses to grab a ruler from my desk, which is covered in a layer of dust that I want to describe as thin but is, in fact, thick. Bordering on "duvet."

"What are you doing?" I say. "Like: redecorating?" Man, it's been ages since I've had a scene partner. My dialogue's rusty.

"I'm measuring your window."

I perk up. "Oh, are we jumping to our deaths?"

Geoff shoots me a straight boy's version of daggers, which are actually more like bullets. Please, like a straight boy would ever knife somebody to death. That would require a degree of closeness I don't think they're genetically capable of. "Dead teenager jokes, Quinn? You, of all people?"

"My timing's off. Sue me."

He ignores me instead, the in-person equivalent of sending a call straight to voice mail. Not that I've been on my cell much these days. Like, at all. "I'm just getting some dimensions," he says, "and then we're going out to buy you that air conditioner."

But I'm barely listening, because now I'm staring past Geoff to the rocky driveway outside, where he and Annabeth and I set up a lemonade stand when we were little. Ugh. I hate that word: *Were*. The only word I hate more than *were* is *was*. Annabeth is so not a past-tense kind of person. Frankly, my sister could be so present, it was intimidating.

I blink hard and kind of hope a zombie apocalypse might really appear: a real-life *Night of the Living Dead* (excellent popcorn flick), except set in the daytime, in our yard. *Somebody bite me, please,* I would yell out the window. But nope. No zombies. It's just that rocky driveway out there, with no lemonade stand in sight.

"All right," Geoff says, "all set." The floor creaks, which must mean he's moving toward the door. I'm on pause, stuck looking outside.

Then: "Hold up," I say. "How much do you think air conditioners cost?"

I'm a little low on cash these days. Last night I had half a Hot Pocket for dinner and a packet of Theraflu for dessert. It actually wasn't so bad. That stuff will knock you *out*.

Geoff's tapping something into his phone. "I dunno. We'll use my mom's card if we have to."

His parents have a nicer house than we do. Actually, ha, everybody does.

Now Geoff's in my bathroom, which never ends well. But when I go to tell him *no*, and to *use the one downstairs*, my shower squeaks on. Plot twist.

"Dammit," I hear him mutter. He scalded his hand, I know it. Our sole luxury around here is instant hot water, and also an agreement that you don't have to make eye contact at the dinner table. Which is actually pretty great.

"Get in," Geoff shouts to me.

"I'm not taking a shower with you," I say—as a *joke*, obviously.

"You wish," he goes, but not in a mean way. Also, we've never really talked about *that*, but I think he knows I do *not* wish. Frankly, there have been really good sandwiches I'd rather lose my virginity to than Geoff. He's not my type.

(I am still narrowing down my type.)

We switch places, and when he's back in my room, I step into the moldy chamber that's also known as my shower.

"I'm giving you two minutes," he says from outside the door.

"Lay off," I call back. "It's not like Pittsburgh is going through a drought."

Geoff pushes the door back open and shakes his head at me. "Quinn, your friggin' *life* has been a drought. And this summer, we're gonna make some rain."

So . . . *yikes*, am I right? I literally spend half my life wanting to rewrite Geoff's taglines.

"Very poetic," I say, covering myself up. "I'd do a slow clap for you, but I don't want to expose my junk."

He rolls his eyes and heads back into my room. I keep trying to think of good excuses to get him out of the house so I can just lie down in the bathtub and maybe try to fall back asleep. But it's been so long since I've engaged in an intellectual debate that stretched beyond "pepperoni or plain" that my brain stalls.

"This is your one-minute warning!" he yells.

I let the water gush into my mouth, and I close my eyes and plug up my ears with my fingers, and in the insistent *tip-tip-tip* on the tin roof of my head, I decide to decide that making some metaphorical rain this summer isn't the worst idea of all time.

Look at me. Attempting optimism.

I make a note to share this with my therapist at the next session. That'll buy me some brownie points. It's funny how I try to piss off my school counselor but try to *impress* my therapist. Throw the word "Doctor" in front of somebody's name and all of a sudden I want her to like me.

"Fifteen seconds!"

Who am I kidding. I want everyone to like me.

"Okay, hang out in the hallway," I say to Geoff. I towel off in my room and throw on a clean-ish pair of shorts and a definitely not clean T-shirt, and then I slip on some Vans and duck my head out to check if he's still there or if I just made this whole thing up. If I'm back to my old ways, naively imagining things will turn out okay, like they do in the movies.

"You ready to jump-start June?" Geoff goes. He's there all right, sitting against the hallway wall, playing a game on his phone and not even pausing to look up. God, his outfits are ridiculous.

God, it's good to see him.

"I guess we'll find out," I say.

He leaps to his feet and pockets his cell.

"Just, be quiet going down the stairs. My mom is sleeping."

I watch his eyes flick over to the buzz mark in my hair, and right when I think he's going to say, *Put a hat on*—because my head really does look like a yard-work accident—instead he just goes, "See you in the car," and he smiles.

That's the thing about best friends: They don't really care what you look like. The real ones don't, anyway.

He clomps down the stairs. He isn't quiet about it at all. Straight boys.

I take one more survey of my room, wondering how it'll feel to return to such a storm of dirty laundry and empty Hot Pocket containers later on today.

"Let's *go*," Geoff whisper-shouts from downstairs.

I've gotta get out of here. Nobody ever talks about the fact that grief's best friend is boredom. Why is that? Why aren't we warning people about this?

"Shotgun," I call back.

CHAPTER TWO

Not to sound like an old lady, but has the outside world always been so loud? Or felt so awkward? For instance, there's maybe nothing more awkward than sitting on a lawn mower in Aisle 4 of a busy Home Depot, without a cell phone to pass the time, while your best friend is off finding an employee. Like: All-time awkwardness record.

"Oh my God, Quinn Roberts."

Scratch that. There *is* something more awkward than all of that. It's being caught doing it.

"Oh, hey," I go. I *knew* this would happen. The zombie apocalypse has arrived, and it's starring Liz Morgan. "How's it going."

Liz was on the pep squad with Annabeth their freshman year. Annabeth wasn't the biggest fan of Liz, but my sister was so plainly decent to everybody that the entire school considered her to be, like, a second-tier friend.

I was third-tier, by association.

"How are *you*?" Liz says, while kind of absentmindedly peeling away a layer of country-club sunburn from her arm. She's first-tier, by the way—and giving me the kind of look you'd give a turtle that's been stuck on its back for six months.

You have to understand: Usually humans forget even the most crippling events if they're not personally inconvenienced themselves. My sister's blazing car blocked the only open exit from school that December afternoon, and thus Liz Morgan and every other student became a kind of victim. Trapped for an extra hour on the last day before winter break. . . .

"Um, I'm okay," I say, remembering to cover the buzz mark in my hair.

Then: "Liz!" Geoff says, reappearing, thank God, and trailed by the kind of Home Depot employee who looks like he majored in Hating Teenagers at some junior college in Ohio.

"Mm, hey," Liz says. She *might* not know Geoff's name. Regardless, I catch him checking her out—though, frankly, Stevie Wonder could probably catch Geoff checking Liz out.

"Uh, is someone buying an air conditioner or not?" the Home Depot employee says, and Liz giggles and covers her mouth and goes, "Well *I'm* not," and then she backs away and takes off like this is the most hilarious and embarrassing mix-up in the history of comedy. Girls, man.

Geoff sighs in her wake. He's never had a girlfriend. I mean, look at his shorts.

The Home Depot guy casually puts his hand on the single most expensive air conditioner out of about a thousand options. "So, how big a room are you cooling off?" he asks me, and I realize I should stand up and pretend to be a human.

"Um." I look at Geoff like maybe *he'll* just sort of intuitively know my bedroom's square footage—his mom is an architect—but then I tell myself to answer this question. Seriously, I go, *Answer the question, Quinn,* to myself. Because maybe answering an easy question like this one will help build my confidence up to the harder ones I'm bound to be getting any day now, like: *Do you think you'll graduate with the rest of the seniors next year?* or, *Are you still planning on making your famous movies now that Annabeth is gone?* or, *Speaking of Annabeth, why didn't you show up to your own sister's memorial?*

"The room's big enough to fit a twin-size bed and eleven pizza boxes," I say to the Home Depot guy, fast, and Geoff busts out laughing in a way that's so musical, it practically borders on "inappropriate underscoring" for the scene we're having.

In other words it's the best song ever.

The employee narrows appropriate AC models down to two, and I blindly point at the one that I think looks the "cutest," God help me, and then Geoff goes, "Let's pay for this thing," and whaps my shoulder pretty hard. I act like it hurts, but it actually feels good. It feels like another person.

We make our way to the parking lot. It is so unbelievably

hot out that I can smell my Speed Stick wafting up like an Alpine fog. Beats the alternative.

"Hey, you did good back there," Geoff says, after we slide the air conditioner box into his trunk. And I do mean *his* trunk. When your dad owns the biggest car dealership in town, you get your own car, and it's not even "pre-owned."

"What do you mean I did good?" I say. "You *bought* this damn thing."

"It was your first time being spotted in public," he goes. "And you didn't even flinch."

He's talking about Liz, of course. But he's wrong: I did flinch. I flinched when I saw Liz clicking her nails against her phone screen, because she has the exact same panda bear phone case that Annabeth has. Had. It's weird how you remember the little details. I don't even remember what I had for lunch yesterday.

"Quinn," Geoff says.

Actually: lie. I had a microwaved burrito and one spoonful of plain yogurt, having mistaken it, tragically, for vanilla.

"Hmm?" I say.

"I said, do you wanna get an icy or something?"

That sounds really good, actually. "Nah," I say. "I think I just want to go install this thing and take a nap. I had a really long night."

Of sleeping, I don't say. A long night of sleeping. Like: thirteen hours. I'm telling you, Theraflu *works*.

"Okay, no problem," Geoff says, unlocking the car doors.

But then his phone *ding*s as we're climbing in, and he checks it, and he grins. Geoff has four distinct grins. This is his "trouble grin."

"What?" I say.

He looks at me. He's still grinning.

"What?"

He turns on the car. "Sorry," he says. "Our plans just changed."

CHAPTER THREE

Forget what I said earlier. Best friends very much do care what you look like. Especially when they are dragging you to your first ever college party, tonight.

"Yeah, you guys, this is going to be tricky to fix."

Meet Zoë Phillips. Geoff and I are in her parents' basement, three neighborhoods over behind the park. Zoë is circling me like she's a trainee witch who's been left alone with the cauldron for the first time.

"You just have to be kinda quick about it," Geoff says to her, "because Quinn and I have to get downtown before traffic hits."

Zoë is a former classmate of ours who got her GED and is going to cosmetology college this fall—*not* "beauty school." Do not call it beauty school in front of her, believe me.

"Just don't do anything too crazy," I say to her. Zoë's own

haircut seems to have been achieved by . . . setting fire to it? Sticking her head into a food processor? Hard to tell.

Zoë gathers most of *my* hair in her hands and then bites her lip. "You've got a lot of nerve," she says, grabbing a strangely large pair of scissors. Like, the kitchen kind. "Demanding miracles after you left the house looking like *this*."

That makes me feel kind of bad. If there's one thing I'm usually not *that* self-conscious about, it's my looks. I even did some modeling when I was little. I mean, just local stuff, but it was still modeling. Apparently there's a whole new thing to question about my life now: if the way I feel inside is actually eroding my shell into something legitimately ugly.

I watch Geoff collapse into this fugly love seat and act like he's having a seizure, just to make me laugh. It works.

"So, big plans tonight, guys?" Zoë says. Her voice is unsteady. A single clip of hair falls to my shoulder. She takes a step back. Here goes everything.

"Just some party," Geoff goes, "at my sister's new place, in Squirrel Hill. Had to make sure Quinn didn't show up looking like a lost bet."

He gives me the thumbs-up in a way that's so earnest, I have to look away. Too much kindness in one day and I might internally combust, or worse: cry.

I don't cry in front of people.

"Cool," Zoë says, in a drone. She gives up on the scissors, reaches for electric clippers, and looks at me in the mirror.

"You ready?" she asks, with a tone that suggests that *she*, in fact, is not ready.

"He's ready," Geoff says, when I realize I haven't answered yet, probably a full thirty seconds later. Perhaps I'm just hypnotized by how hard Zoë's hands are shaking.

I could have just given *myself* a buzz cut, of course, but at least Geoff got to hang out around a real live girl for twenty minutes (he's never really "been" with a girl). Anyway, that's the most optimistic way I can frame my new haircut. And believe me— they all got cut, every one of them. Picture a cue ball with lips.

Geoff's tapping his fingers against his steering wheel and humming, attempting to "add harmonies" to a song on the radio that's in an entirely different key. When he makes a surprise right out of Zoë's parents' subdivision, I use the moment as an excuse to crank down the volume.

"Wait, why aren't we going left?" I ask. "Why are we taking the parkway?"

Geoff keeps drumming right along, still hearing a song that I'm not. "I thought we'd take the long way. To, like, avoid going past the school."

Oh. That's pretty thoughtful of him.

"Oh."

Geoff knows I still haven't been back, not since the day before Christmas break, and so I still haven't seen the guardrail that Annabeth crashed into, headfirst, dying "instantly or close to instantly." Those were the last words I heard about her final moments, after the principal himself ducked into my health class and pulled me into the hall and told me he had some "difficult news" for me. I was sure it was going to be about my mom—I'm always stressing out about her health, because of her weight—but no, it was Annabeth: "Your sister, Quinn, has been in an accident, Quinn." I'll never forget that, the way the principal said my name twice in the same sentence, before he explained how Annabeth had run the red light at the bottom of the hill outside school. How she had gotten sideswiped and spun on the ice into the guardrail. How, incidentally, she had died "instantly or close to instantly." And right then, I smelled the smoke from her car.

That's the same day I started wearing earplugs. That's the same night I gave up on becoming a screenwriter, or an anythingwriter, or an anything.

"Well, maybe we can drive by it sometime later this summer," I say to Geoff. He's still tapping his hands. This generic brass-and-fake-leather bracelet he always wears is adding annoying tambourine sounds.

"Sure thing," he goes, "but, just a heads-up: There's this, like, weird portrait of Annabeth painted on the side of the school now."

"Okay?" I'm not following.

"The principal had the middle schoolers do it. As a spring art project tribute thing."

"Okay?" He's stalling. "And?" There's always an *and* with Geoff.

He pulls onto the parkway. "Dude: Your sister kind of ended up looking like a . . . like a giant *pug*."

Somehow, this makes me laugh. If *you* think I'm a confusing person, imagine actually *being* me.

"Why are you laughing?"

"That's just ridiculous with a side of ridiculous," I go, opening his glove compartment to get a Jolly Rancher, which is melted beyond oblivion. "It sounds like a straight-to-DVD Disney release: *My Sister, the Pug*."

Oof. No reaction. That can't be good. People used to say I was witty. The guy who could find the funny in any situation.

"*Any*way," I go.

It's quiet for a little while, and when I reach to adjust the volume back up, I catch Geoff wiping his nose against his arm. I should be the one crying, but I'm not. It never dawns on me that as an American, you're legally allowed to cry in front of others. Maybe I've just seen too many old movies. Tough guys never cry in old movies.

"Hey, actually—can you get off at the next exit?" I say. "I should swing home for a sec. I wanna put on a clean shirt for the party."

"Quinn, we both know you don't have any clean shirts."

"Ha."

I'm thinking of so many mean things I could say about his "mustache."

I punch his arm, instead, and his car swerves, which

makes my stomach nervous. My stomach is like a weather vane. It knows what I'm feeling before I do, always. Maybe that's why I've been the emotional equivalent of a Hot Pocket for half a year. "I might not have any clean shirts," I say, "but my dad does."

"D'okay," Geoff says, using his turn signal like the responsible young man he apparently turned into during my recent absence.

"I'll be two seconds," I say, when he pulls into our rocky driveway with no lemonade stand in sight. But he doesn't stay in the car. He follows me right up the front steps, and right into our foyer, and right past the powder room with the broken toilet seat, until we find Mom—with her head in the freezer like she's an ostrich who couldn't find any suitable sand.

"Babe?" Mom says, pulling her beautiful face out. Seriously, she's beautiful. Fact. "Where did you go?" She shuts the freezer door. "And what happened to your gorgeous *hair*?"

That's a stretch. My former hair was about as gorgeous as bathwater after a bath, after a rugged hike. My current haircut is, at least, practically see-through.

"It's the new trend, Ma," I say, running my hand over the stubble. "All the cool kids are doing it."

"Well . . . at least I get to see that handsome *face* again."

"Hi, Mrs. R.!" Geoff says, pushing past me and giving Mom the kind of hug people write songs about.

"Geoffrey, Geoffrey, look at you. A regular man."

Geoff feigns a whole aw-shucks routine, but you can tell he's secretly thrilled to be getting attention from a female, any female.

Mom reaches her hand forward and tries wiping Geoff's upper lip. "You've got something there, Geoffrey," she says, and he pulls back and hops up to sit on our counter, where he attempts to say with a totally straight face: "It's a mustache, Mrs. R."

But that just turns Mom into an instant giggle machine. It is so good to hear her feeling good about something.

"Sure it is, Geoffrey," she says, winking at me. "Sure it's a mustache."

I take off. "Geoff and I are hanging tonight"—backing out of the kitchen before she can put up a fight that I didn't ask for her permission first—"so I'm gonna throw on a clean shirt."

Wait for it. Waaait for it.

But she doesn't put up a fight or say I can't go. She just looks at Geoff and right away both of their eyes are watery, like it's been their big secret plan all along to get me out of the house. Which, who knows, maybe it has been.

"Call me if you're going to be later than eleven!" Mom yells when I'm hopping up the stairs three steps at a time. Six months of inactivity have suddenly turned me into a well-rested iron man.

"You bet!" I yell back.

Except my phone isn't charged. It isn't even plugged in.

I don't even know where it is, to be honest, because I sort of blocked that day out. I haven't turned my phone on since the accident, when I figured out why Annabeth got into the accident to begin with, dying "instantly or nearly instantly," as if the timing of somebody's death matters. They're dead. Roll the credits.

I ransack Dad's old closet to try and find his least offensive shirt. It's a delicate proposition: This is my first college party, and I agreed to go only because it's a group of people who don't know anything about my past, and won't look at me like I'm the only surviving seabird after a devastating oil spill.

Also, there's going to be beer.

But the Asshole Formerly Known As Dad's shirts always tended toward Hawaiian prints and polyester button-ups. These are not the shirts of a man who owns the area's number-one car dealership or hugs his kids. These are the shirts of a shifty junior manager who walks out on his wife on her birthday. I'm stuck.

I give up and go to Dad's shelf in the medicine cabinet, grabbing some okay-looking Polo cologne and giving my T-shirt a solid five pumps, figuring three of them should mellow out by the time we show up to the party.

"You kids done catching up?" I say from the bottom step, rounding my way into the kitchen like everything's normal again.

But I don't think they heard me, because they're . . .

whimpering? No—because they're whimpering, period. Mom is holding Geoff and rocking him a little bit, each of them acting out the very scene I still haven't had with her myself yet.

I study my shoes and pull off a pretty good pretend cough. "Let's go," I say. "Before traffic gets bad."

CHAPTER FOUR

W e're on the street outside Geoff's sister's place in Squirrel Hill, looking up at a couple of big-shot college kids who are leaning out a window, smoking. I had the bright idea to stop and pick up something "nice" for the party, so when someone finally buzzes us in and we trudge up the four floors (without an elevator), I count it as a minor set-back when a girl in a fedora swings open the door, looks at what I've brought, and calls back to the group: "Great. Another hummus."

"Dude, let's go in," Geoff says.

The place is awesome. Like, I can't believe in a couple of years I could actually live like this. You know, if I start doing my homework again and actually apply to college, ha.

"We don't have to stay long," Geoff says. Now we're standing just inside his sister's doorway, at the beginning of a long hallway that hopefully leads to unlimited fun. And beer. Tonight is The Night I Try Beer and Maybe Pot.

"It's cool," I go, noticing a tea-colored stain in the ceiling. "I'll be okay."

"I actually *can't* stay that late, to be honest," Geoff goes, starting to lead me toward a room that's boomeranging with voices. "I have the first shift at Loco Mocha tomorrow."

"Wait, you got a *job?*" I go. I stop him beside a bathroom that's got this giant Yankee Candle going. Classy place.

"Yeah, I got a job," Geoff goes. "Turn on your phone sometime. It will deliver mysterious things to you, like news."

"No, I just can't believe *you* got a job."

We used to make movies together, every day, all day, every summer. I'd write them, Annabeth would direct, Geoff would star. He was a terrible actor. So terrible it was funny, and somehow seemed like a version of good.

"My *dad* made me get a job."

"But your dad is, like . . ." I consider how to phrase this. Geoff and I don't talk about money. He just . . . pays for stuff, while I look away. "Loaded."

Geoff laughs, heads into the bathroom, and swishes with Listerine right out of his sister's bottle. Straight boys, every last one of 'em a mystery.

Anyway, he's back. "We do fine, but we are not exactly *loaded*. That's just what people think."

"You drive a brand-new Toyota, Geoff."

"You don't know anything about cars, Quinny. It's not exactly a Tesla."

"What's that?"

"Exactly."

We keep walking. It is a seriously long hallway, made emptier by how there's nothing in it but us, no furniture or posters or anything. I can't believe college kids can afford a place with such a long hallway.

"Well, whatever," Geoff goes. "My dad said that in order to 'learn money, you've got to earn money.' So, like I said. Whatever."

These must be the lessons other kids get from their dads. Here is the lesson I got: When your wife turns forty, run for the hills and don't take your shorts.

"Maybe *I* should get a job at Loco this summer," I start to say—it could be fun to make coffee all day—but Geoff's big sister, Carly, appears at the end of the hallway, puts her hands on her hips, and openly examines our outfits. Carly herself looks as if she was standing outside an Urban Outfitters when a pipe bomb went off.

"Jesus, bro," she says, clucking at Geoff, "are you *still* getting dressed in the dark?" She's majoring in Fashion Merchandising, if that helps.

"Ha-ha, Carly," Geoff goes, punching her shoulder harder than guys our age should. Carly's always ripping on Geoff, but she loves the dude. Can't blame her. I mean, the mustache alone gives Geoff a Make-A-Wish vibe that you have to kind of fall for, in a strictly platonic way.

"At least Quinny-boy had the decency to dress in neutrals tonight," Carly goes, bypassing Geoff and giving me a huge hug. My arms don't know how to manage a hug anymore. "Wow," Carly says, coughing, "neutrals and *cologne*, Quinn. Neutrals and cologne."

I pull back and lift my collar to smell myself. "Too much?"

"No," Carly says, running her hand over my head. "People will be too distracted by the hot new military man here to notice that he fell into a vat of Polo."

"Aw, whatevs."

"Seriously, Quinn: You look handsome as *whoa*. You look like a *man*."

Geoff disappears into the montage of bodies just beyond, and I feel my heart kick into gear. Call it little-brother syndrome. I'm desperate for my own independence and then can't stand it when I get it.

I decide I could use that beer. I look like a man. Men drink beer.

"Come on," Carly goes, taking my hand, "let's get you a Sprite."

Great.

She leads me into the living room, where some people are sitting on a picnic blanket in the corner and lighting up what I'm sure is a joint. I've never smoked one myself, not that I wouldn't, necessarily. It's just, when you're third-tier at school, you don't exactly hit the party rounds.

But I'm not third-tier here. I'm no-tier. I'm nobody. It's perfect.

"It's hot as *balls* in here," some guy shouts from the couch.

Carly hands me a 7UP (not Sprite—and yes, there's a difference), and some girl goes, "I love this song," and pulls up the "hot as balls" guy (temperature, not looks; like, definitely *not* my type) from the couch, and they start dancing around a little. The guy's got moves, but the girl is all elbows and knees, and I find myself staring at these mystical college people in a way that might be bordering on stalker-ish if I'm not careful.

"You look like a stalker, Quinn," Geoff says, sneaking up and holding out a little plate of carrots.

"Jesus," I say, "are you off to feed a bunny or something?"

Geoff laughs too hard (it wasn't that great a line) and thrusts the plate at me. "No, dude, I just figured you probably hadn't had any fruits and vegetables since, like, the holidays. I've seen your freezer."

I snort, but he isn't wrong. My mom's theory—which I *fully* endorse—is that fruits are best in a cobbler and vegetables are best in the ground. And yet—and yet!—I've got that crazy-skinny metabolism on my side. But calm down, because I don't mean the ripped kind of skinny. The only six-pack I've got is a case of Sprite I keep in the back of my mini-fridge for special occasions.

It's still a full six-pack. It's been a while since I've had a special occasion.

"Play it again, Car!" the dancing girl calls over to Carly, who's DJ'ing from her iPhone, and Geoff leans in and goes, "Isn't it funny that college kids aren't that much more mature than we are?"

And here I'm thinking they look a full ten *years* older, and probably know to spritz only two pumps of cologne and not five. But I nod and go, "Yeah, I was just thinking that too."

"Song of the summer," Geoff says, and I squinch up my face as he bops his head toward his sister. "This song," Geoff says, explaining modern life to me as if I'm a recently thawed caveman. "Song of the summer."

"Oh, right," I go. But I have no idea. Not a single one, not a clue. I am as clueless about current pop culture as my mom is about current health trends. I'm a classic film buff, which is just about everything about me that's buff.

I'm not proud of this, by the way. It's just an is. Other things I'm not proud of that just are include:

—When I hear recordings of me speaking, I've got a thicker Pittsburghese accent than I or probably anyone would like.

—When the dentist asks me if I floss every day, I sort of chortle and go, "Ch'yah," but I don't, guys.

—When I'm about to do something that makes me nervous, I imagine how the ideal screenplay version of events would play out. As in: I wish my life were a screenplay that I could write. Because if you leave it all up to fate, who knows how your movie's going to turn out? So far mine's a fairly standard coming-of-age LGBT genre film, with a somewhat macabre horror twist. But if it starts veering toward romantic comedy, somebody just murder me.

Obviously I would have made Annabeth direct the film of my life. She was such a good director. She could get compelling performances out of our neighborhood *dogs*, and she did, no sweat. . . .

Jesus, I'm sweating. I must look like such a high school brat, the only person here not holding a red cup. What's with the red cups.

The designated smoking window across the room is unoccupied, and I could use some breeze action, but before I make it over there, Carly pauses the music and shouts: "We're going to the roof! There's a surprise waiting there!"

Big cheers.

I scan the crowd for Geoff but don't see him. Carly's going, "Don't kill each other on the way up, and don't stomp, because our landlady will freak out on us," but nobody's listening. The whole world loves surprises. You tell a group of people they're about to get a surprise, and watch out.

"I hate surprises," I say, to nobody, following the herd and touching my haircut.

CHAPTER FIVE

At the top of three more sets of stairs, I am heaving for breath and thinking that maybe "iron man" was stretching it as a character description for myself, earlier.

Carly slams through a hulking metal door and a gush of wind makes the crowd go "Ahhhhh" in a big choral way. A couple of girls even throw on some harmony, and I'm thinking they must be theater majors, but I'm not thinking it for long—because despite the glare of the rooftop sun backlighting the Cathedral of Learning and a hundred miles of hills over our city's three awkwardly named rivers, I spot Geoff immediately. In fact, it's like the whole scene stops, in order to re-buffer. Geoff is standing dead center on the roof, holding maybe fifty colorful balloons.

What the hell, right?

"Okay, guys, so, listen up," Carly says. "Everybody go to

my baby brother and grab a single balloon and then just sort of like spread out."

Suddenly all I want to be is in college.

I'm one of the last people to get to Geoff, and he hands me a pink balloon, and I go, "Come on, you know my favorite color is green," which makes Geoff laugh, because he knows my least favorite color is green. Sometimes you see the easy sitcom laugh sitting there and you just have to snatch it up.

He and I find a place in the corner. It's a good thing the whole roof is bordered by a kind of old-fashioned guardrail, painted over with a billion layers of black. Enough of these undergrads are tipsy now that I'm glad I won't have to watch some well-groomed drunk kid fall to his or her death tonight.

NEW RULE: I only want to know one person per sixteen years who dies. So, watch out for falling pianos, thirty-two-year-old Quinn.

Geoff's sister stands on a crate and rallies the crowd to look at her. Whistling, clapping, the works.

"So, this is something I used to do at the end of camp every year, and it's amazing."

A few guys in khaki pants and these weirdly starched shirts start jovially pushing one another, hard enough that one of them falls into a girl, who spills beer all over her own tank top. I step forward to help the girl up, to grab the red cup she dropped, to rescue the situation, and it comes to me: Maybe instead of getting a job this summer, I'll just be the superhero boy who rescues girls from finance majors.

"Don't let your balloon go yet!" Geoff goes, gripping my hand in his own strong fist. I don't remember him being strong. This is the June where I've become "handsome as *whoa*" (not my words) and Geoff has become strong.

"Now that we've all pulled ourselves together," Carly goes, not so much shouting now as letting the audience come to her. (Classic technique. There is nothing more frightening than how charming and civilized Anthony Hopkins is in *The Silence of the Lambs*, which was shot here in Pittsburgh, not incidentally.) "Here's the game: I want everyone to think of three things that happened this year that they wished had gone differently," Carly says. And then: "They're allowed to be really sad!"

Oh.

Geoff puts his hand on my shoulder, and I flinch it away, fast, like I'm deflecting a moth or a bee. And in the flinch I suddenly know what this is. This is for me. All of this.

My mom must've known Geoff was going to take me out tonight, or else she would have put up a bigger fuss about me leaving her alone after dark. I'm not third-tier tonight. I'm not even first-tier. I'm the only tier.

This makes me incredibly nervous.

"Does everybody have three things they wish they could just let go of?" Carly says, and nobody says anything, which means they do. When nobody makes a single noise, it means they've never been concentrating harder on something. "On the count of three," Carly goes, "I want everybody to let go of their balloons. Are you with me?"

The crowd smiles so hard, you can actually feel the wind change course. I've learned to semi-believe in stuff like this. The butterfly effect that says if fifty people smile at once, the power of their acne-pocked cheeks can change the wind, if not the world. A wind that has suddenly appeared on this stifling night like the superhero I'd never actually get cast as, not this summer or any summer.

"And after you let your balloon go," Carly says—yup, she's still talking!—"I want you to picture the number-one worst thing that happened to you this year, and I want you to watch it float away until you can't see it anymore." She pauses. "Everybody close your eyes. This is what we did at camp." As if this last tidbit legitimizes the whole enterprise.

"Close your eyes, Quinny," Geoff says.

And so I do, to humor him. And I earnestly try to think about the worst thing that happened to me this year. And, instead, I come up with a riddle: How terrible of a guy do you have to be if the worst thing you can think of *isn't* that you lost your sister, but that you lost yourself?

But then Carly goes, "One," and by the time she gets to "three," everybody's saying it with her. Even I am caught up in the moment to such a degree that I dare myself to imagine this turning into a perfect screenplay sequence, just like I did in the old days.

EXT. CARLY'S ROOF IN SQUIRREL HILL - NIGHT

Quinn and the college kids let their balloons
go, watching as they turn from fifty separate
shapes into fifty little Skittles until,
finally, the balloons become a single rubber
star full of all the kids' regrets from this
past year.

Quinn smiles. When was the last time he smiled
so big? He's just so relieved to watch his
biggest demon float away into the sky -- so
relieved to mark this moment as the one in
which he can start over.

The crowd cheers. Geoff high-5's Quinn.
Somebody else hands him a beer.

                    QUINN
          Thanks!

                    SEMI-CUTE COLLEGE GUY
          No problem, man! You're gonna
          love it!

    Except, no. Not so much. Because real life doesn't work

like the movies—just ask Marilyn Monroe or James Dean. And so as everyone else around me *does* watch their balloons turn to Skittles, and then into forgotten regrets, I am instead looking three feet ahead at the black guardrail—at *my* balloon, flapping frantically, its pink string caught by the wind in the railing.

The tipsy masses make their way downstairs, in ten seconds or ten minutes, I can't tell. I'm just standing here, with Geoff next to me, staring at my almost comically stuck balloon. *Almost* comically.

When I finally turn to leave for good, and head down to the street, I see something directly across from me on the other side of the roof. Apparently another person's balloon, a green one, became tangled in the railing too.

Another guy's, actually.

The sun is directly behind his head now, giving this guy the look of both the oldest and youngest person you've ever seen, his features the kind of ageless blur that Geoff's mom paid good money to achieve at the plastic surgeon, after his dad cheated on her with *both* receptionists at the car dealership last October. Long story.

"I'll see you downstairs, Quinny," Geoff whispers. "Don't, like, read into the balloon thing. . . ." But his voice trails off. He dragged me here tonight. Geoff planned this out with Carly. He believes in signs and so I have to, too. Best friend law.

"Okay, I'm coming," I say, but then I don't. I take my house keys out of my pocket and I step forward and I pop the pink balloon, *BAM!*, and watch it fall to my feet in a pathetic little zigzag.

I whip around. The sun is almost set. The other guy is still here, though, and has turned from blurry edges to pencil-sharp lines—drawn to be my exact height and size, but with a confident smirk that says he's never lost anything more than a round of cards.

"Nice haircut," he goes, grabbing the door and holding it for me before it slams shut.

And suddenly I know exactly what my type is.

CHAPTER SIX

Y ou okay in there, Quinny?"

I've spent so much time swishing with Listerine that when I finally exit Carly's bathroom, my tongue is basically tingling to the point of numbness. In immediate hindsight: not recommended.

"We should hit the road," Geoff says, crunching a red cup in his hand. I grab it from him and take a swig.

"Ew," I say, "it's warm." I hate warm Coke.

"And even worse . . . ," he goes. Jesus Christ. It's warm Pepsi. Geoff knows how I feel about non-Coke products. "But Carly ran out to get more beer."

My eyes must flicker back to the living room, because Geoff breaks into his conspiracy grin and goes, "I can't believe *I'm* the one trying to leave and you're the one trying to stay. The King of the Loners reinvents himself."

"No, it's just . . ."

Say it, Quinn. Tell him you might have your first genuine crush. I am making up for all categories of lost time tonight. I was the last kid in my class to go through puberty. I want to see the roof guy naked. There, I said it.

"... like ..."

"You haven't been out of the house in six months," Geoff says, for me, "and so you wanna go a little bananas tonight?"

Relief. Close enough. "Exactly that."

"Well, then," Geoff says, "let's spike your 7UP with some vodka."

I don't even know if 7UP and vodka go together, but we skip back to the living room like Girl Scouts on an important mission.

"We're baaaaaack," a voice rings out from behind us, in the epic front hallway that thinks it's a tunnel. Carly and the rooftop guy reappear together.

And the rooftop guy, if anyone missed that.

I stand up straight and try to smile in a way that seems "casual but approachable" (literally I'm directing myself), but the rooftop guy totally doesn't notice me at all. Maybe he actually *hated* my haircut. Maybe he's majoring in Irony. Worse: Maybe he's straight.

"Okay, so Amir had this idea for a game we can play," Carly goes, stepping past us and setting two six-packs of Iron City down on a coffee table that is fashioned, somewhat improbably, out of an old aquarium.

But who has time for details. Rooftop guy has a name. Amir. Now, that's a hell of a name. Strong, simple, super masculine. The very opposite of *Quinn*.

The partygoers are scattering around me, hunting for scraps of paper. Geoff is waving his hands in my face. They smell like hummus. "Earth to Quinn," he goes.

"Uh-huh."

"Have you ever played Celebrity?"

"If I haven't played it with you, no. So: no."

"It's fun."

"Okay," Carly says, "if you're a native Pittsburgher, you're on my team. And if you're from out of town, you're on Amir's!"

Shouting and uproar. The "hot as balls" guy from earlier (not my type; not my Amir, ha) announces he's from Wheeling, West Virginia, so the out-of-town team "needs to come over here," he goes, "because I'm not leaving the couch." Instantly Amir's team crashes onto the sofa in a tight pack: a group of wolves not bred in Pittsburgh.

"Native Pittsburghers," Carly says, adopting the longest, ugliest version of our local dialect that you can imagine, "let's just sit by the TV." (If you don't know anyone from Pittsburgh, look it up on YouTube. You won't believe it. Our accent sounds something like a parrot doing an impression of a fire alarm.)

"Wait, the teams are uneven," says a non-native. "You guys have two too many."

"Quinny's not from Pittsburgh!" Geoff offers, unbelievably. "He's from Cleveland."

"Uh, we moved down here when I was, like, *one*," I say.

But Carly holds up her hands and does a big "Rules are rules!" thing, and I am so frustrated because the last thing I want is to be on Amir's team. I'm not ready to join forces. I don't even know how to play this game.

Geoff smiles at me like we're in on the same running joke that is my life. We are not.

I sit on the floor next to the couch. Somebody hands me five torn-up slips of notebook paper, and I go, "Thanks," and when I'm sitting here long enough without doing anything, this girl literally furrows her brow like Faye Dunaway in *Mommie Dearest* and goes, "Can't think of anyone?"

I clear my throat. "Um."

"Just write down five celebrities," she says.

You have to see *Mommie Dearest*, by the way. Oh my God. Put it on the list.

"On the pieces of paper," she continues. "One celebrity for each paper." She holds out a pen and looks at me like I'm a dangerous alien in neutral clothes. Which, let's be honest.

Carly's kicking off her sandals. "Okay, does everybody have their celebrities?"

Somebody volunteers his Pirates hat to be used as the "bowl" for us to put our slips of paper into, and that's when

Faye Dunaway says, louder than you'd believe: "Wait. The cute kid hasn't written down his names yet."

I mean, at least she thinks I'm cute.

"Oh, you can go without me," I say, but a tipsy guy from the Pittsburgh team goes, "No way. It *has* to be even numbers! It *has* to be." As if party games are known for their fairness. As if that's the chief quality that gets people hooked on the party game circuit.

Geoff and I lock eyes, and he breaks into the biggest "I'm sorry" grin I've seen since the time in elementary school he let it slip to the other boys that I'd "borrowed" two of Carly's Barbies after a sleepover; he's clearly remembering, only now, how completely out of the loop I am about current pop culture.

"*Bro*, just think of five famous people," a guy from my team says, and so I take the pen from Faye Dunaway and like a magic wand it supplies me with insight: I'll use my practically genetic aversion to being ordinary to my advantage.

1. Hitchcock. 2. Kubrick. 3. Mankiewicz. 4. Preminger. And, for the modern crowd: 5. Tarantino. Yes. *Yes*. Filmmaker celebrities for the ages.

I'm writing so fast that somebody actually goes: "The kid's on fire!" and I fold my sheets of paper in half and drop them in the Pirates hat. Carly claps her hands together. It's all good.

"Okay, anyone who hasn't played before: It's like, I don't know, verbal charades, and your team has to guess who you're acting out—"

"And you only get a minute each, *no cheating*," Geoff goes. He cracks his knuckles and punches his fist into his hand, acting all mock competitive. It makes me laugh. This is going to be *fine*.

"First round!" Carly goes, grabbing the hat. "My house, my rules. Devon, you're up."

Somebody offers to time the rounds on their phone, and we're off.

"Okay," Devon says, looking at her first slip of paper and bouncing up and down a little. "Wait, can I, like, pass?"

"Fifty seconds left!" the timer from the other team says. I dare myself to glance at Amir. He is the only person on our team looking at Devon with a small smile on his face—a face that's distinguished by this jawline you could open a manila envelope with. Anyway, whatever. His little smile. It is the sweetest thing. Everybody else is teasing Devon for being so stuck on the first round. But Amir is smiling, smiling. The kind of smile you have to name twice.

"Time!" the timekeeper calls, and Devon slaps her hands down and goes, "I didn't even know who it *was*! It was like a long Russian name or something!" She shows the paper to us and somebody from the other team kicks her in the butt and says, "No cheating!" and she falls onto the floor and puts her feet against the aquarium and sighs.

"Let's go in order of birthdays," someone suggests. "Like, whoever's birthday is next should just go."

A Pittsburgh guy goes, "My birthday's on Tuesday!" and a bunch of girls go, "Aww, Josh!" like he just admitted he's not actually a human guy but in fact fifteen puppies in a tank top. Josh gets up and takes the hat and suddenly the game gets *serious*, though I'm not really thinking about that. I'm thinking about the fact that my birthday is this coming Sunday.

"*Go.*"

Josh grabs the first celebrity. "Okay, he owns like a million buildings and has crazy hair that looks like a frittata!"

"Donald Trump!"

Josh doesn't even say *yes*; he just throws the clue down and we non-natives moan but also secretly love that now we're all *about* something, together.

LIFE HACK: That's all anyone ever wants.

"Okay," Josh goes, "he used to be, like, the biggest movie star ever when our parents were our age, but then he went crazy."

"Tom Cruise!"

"No!"

"John Travolta!"

"Yes!"

Ugh. Biggest movie star ever? Marlon Brando much?

Whatever. Next. Josh twists a piece of hair between his fingers, and he's starting to sweat, and this is the most cardio-intense party game I've ever seen. "Okay," Josh goes, "*You get a car, and you get a car, and you get a car.*"

The Pittsburghers erupt into laughter and everybody

shouts, "Oprah!"—even my team does—and oh my God wait till they get to one of my names and are blown away that the cute kid is actually a mature man.

"Okay," Josh goes, trying not to laugh, "I think he was, like, a famous mime."

"Time!" Carly calls out. She's boogying around and eating some of the hummus that I brought. Nobody seems to mind the fact that I brought "another hummus" now. Life can be so weird.

"Who's up? Who's up?" somebody goes, and since I don't have a phone to pretend I'm getting a text, I fake a big yawn.

"Quinny, your birthday's on Sunday, right?"

I am going to kill Geoff.

"Birthday boy! Birthday boy!" He attempts to start a chant. Fail.

I get up and wonder how sweaty my butt looks in my shorts and if I'll recognize a single celebrity name, and I pray pray pray I pick one of my own. I know just how to act out Hitchcock. Please: Crouch like birds are attacking, shriek like you're being stabbed in a shower, easy.

"Okay, *time*," Carly says, for the first time not sounding excited but rather cautious. Can't blame her there. I literally have no idea who the first celebrity is.

"Oh, jeez."

See, this is why I like everything written out beforehand. I am trying to star in my life story, not appear as the unbilled comic sidekick.

"Say something," a girl from my team says. "Say anything."

Amir and I catch eyes and dammit I look away.

"Is it a man or a woman?" says Faye Dunaway.

"I think a man."

"Oh, *Christ*."

"I mean—sorry—definitely a guy."

"Thirty seconds!" Carly says.

"Okay," I say, "his last name is, like, French."

"Gérard Depardieu!" a teammate says, and I appreciate, at least, the relatively obscure movie star reference.

"No, but really good guess."

"Thanks. I don't need positive reinforcement, I need *clues*."

Yikes.

"*Guys*, back off," Carly goes, but oh God: I don't want to be that kid who everyone has to be nice to because their parents got a handout at the beginning of the year saying their child would be sharing the classroom with "someone exceptional."

"Oh!" I say. I swing my arms so wide that it knocks an entire liter of Fanta into a bowl of corn chips. Worth it. "His last name is like Pepé Le Pew. You know, the, like, possum cartoon thing."

"He was a *skunk*," a girl says, wiping Fanta from her leg. You could say it kind of splashed "everywhere."

"And his first name is Italian!" I go.

"*Time!*" Carly hollers. Big hoots from the Pittsburgh team, who are up three-nothing. Josh is literally still getting high-fives for the John Travolta/Oprah sequence.

"Pepé Le Pew was a *skunk*," that girl says again, in case I didn't hear her, which I did.

"Well, who *was* it?" asks my "hot as balls" teammate, who never even tried to guess during my round, not even once.

"I thought we weren't showing clues," I say, but *now* nobody puts up a fight, and so I hold up the celebrity for him to see.

"Mario *Lemieux*?" he goes. "You don't know who Mario *Lemieux* is?"

"One of the most legendary Penguins of all time," somebody else adds.

Ugh. A hockey reference. The clue might as well have been written upside down, in Arabic.

"Jesus, you call yourself a Pittsburgher?"

"No." I sit down. "I'm from Cleveland."

The "hot as balls" guy leans forward. Now I see what he's doing. He's impressing this girl next to him. "You could have literally just said, 'This guy's first name was one of the most iconic Nintendo characters of all time.'"

I try not to scrunch my eyebrows at him, but *whoops*.

"Super *Mario* Brothers," he goes. "Hello? Are you secretly *ninety*?"

The girl next to him giggles and whaps his shoulder in a "You big lug" kind of way. They are definitely doing it later tonight.

I hug my knees. I am the last American virgin.

"So, whose birthday is next?" Carly tries to say, but it's as if the soundman forgot to turn on her microphone; that's the effect her prompt has. Nothing.

I get up to take the ruined corn chips to the kitchen—also to launch an investigation into whether my face is incredibly hot or incredibly cold (it's one or the other)—and as I set the bowl in the sink, a spider crawls out from beneath the window-sill and startles me enough that I back up, hard, into somebody.

"Sorry," I say. With my luck, it's probably the girl whose bright white jeans were splashed with Fanta.

Nope. It's worse.

"No problem."

It's Amir. We made actual physical contact and I didn't even have the benefit of experiencing it face-to-face.

I mumble something and duck my head down, side-stepping out of the kitchen, taking great notice of the floor, of exquisite dust bunnies and a fascinating paper clip, of any-thing but up.

"We should go," Geoff says, when I nearly crash into him, too. "First shift at Loco Mocha."

But that's not what he's saying, or what he's meaning, any-way. *"The minute we got your air conditioner today,"* is what he's really saying, *"we should have just gone back to install it and never let you leave home again."*

That's the one dangerous thing about having a best friend. You can always tell when they're glad not to be you.

CHAPTER SEVEN

We have to pull off of I-79 because Geoff's Corolla is running super low on gas. Usually he just fills it up for free at his dad's dealership—did you know car dealerships have their own on-site gas stations? I didn't—so tonight Geoff is in his version of a pissy mood because he actually has to pay to refill his tank.

Geoff's version of pissy is still pretty optimistic.

"Hey, Quinny," he says, sticking his head through the driver's window from outside. "Can you pump for a second? I actually really have to take a leak."

Sure. I unbuckle and walk around and take the nozzle from him, and when he stumbles away a little bit, I go, "Are you, like, sober enough to drive?" and he goes, "*Now* you ask me," which isn't exactly an answer.

It's been a while since I've pumped gas. Annabeth drove our only car, that day. We haven't gotten it replaced.

"Holy shit, Quinn Roberts," I hear. Even though the pump clicks off at that very moment, my hand reflexively turns back into a fist, clamping it back on. Auto-fists are what auto-happen whenever I hear Blake Thompson's voice.

"Hey, Blake," I go, unclenching my hand.

"Hey," he goes.

I turn to see which kind of face he's making at me. It's always a face with Blake Thompson, but it's his arms that I zero in on. They're overflowing with snack foods—Utz chips and Mountain Dews, you get the idea.

"You want one of these?" he goes. Apparently I'm staring at a Clark Bar.

"No, it's cool," I go, and then Geoff's flip-flops are *s-lapping* back across the parking lot. He gets in front of me like he's a mother lioness.

"Need something, Thompson?" Geoff goes. I slink away and open the passenger-side door and just stand behind it as if it's a shield.

"No, we're good," Blake says. He turns abruptly toward his truck, and as he does a Sierra Mist falls out of his arms. It rolls onto Geoff's foot. Geoff tosses it into Blake's pickup truck window for him, and Blake takes off without saying anything else, his truck belching smoke, one of his rear taillights blinking like a carnival.

We're pulling out of the gas station and are a full one minute back into the trip before Geoff goes, "Buckle up"—my mom was always strangely lax about making us buckle up—and then, "That was weird back there."

I know what he means but I don't, either. "Yeah," I say.

"Did Blake give you shit when I was inside?"

"No," I say, opening Geoff's glove compartment for a Jolly Rancher. He's out of my favorite flavor, but I'll persevere. "No, he didn't give me shit at all. He was oddly nice."

"Well, that's cool," Geoff goes, turning onto my driveway without using the turn signal. Thank God. It was beginning to bother me how conscientious Geoff has been seeming.

"Yeah," I say, but I'm not thinking it was cool. I'm thinking I wish Blake *had* been a total jagoff to me, back in the Marathon Gas parking lot off I-79, because then we'd be back to how life was before December twentieth. Blake Thompson being nice to anybody means they are permanently in the leper category—officially not worth picking on.

I am now the guy people pity. Don't pity me, people! Make fun of my haircut. My dad's cologne, even. Treat me like you treat everybody.

"You wanna get out?" Geoff says, because I guess I'm just sitting here in the driveway, buckled up, looking at the birch tree where Annabeth and I tied the stray dog we were so excited to find, which Dad didn't let us keep.

I've got a Hefty bag out and I'm filling it with three expired Healthy Choices at a time. Then I'm on my knees, twisting open jars of cinnamon applesauce and trying to figure out if anything in the fridge is still edible. QUESTION: Can jelly grow mold? (ANSWER: It can!)

I'm not being that quiet about any of this, either. Mom's upstairs in her room watching her stories on full blast, so I should be good.

Ten minutes and two full Hefty bags later I've moved on to confronting our pantry, which is also where Dad kept this big animal-cracker barrel for loose coins. It's the most unlikely thing ever, sitting there on the top shelf. In order to put your spare change into it, you have to get out the step stool—which is missing its top ladder rung—and balance on the top without falling and dying. And so we never do.

If this isn't a metaphor for the Roberts family's approach to "savings," I don't know what is.

Oops, never mind about me not disturbing Mom. I hear her door swing open upstairs and these gravelly voices from her police procedurals filling the stairwell. It's actually nice to have a man's voice in the house again.

Surprise: Here she comes.

"Hi, Mama," I say when she steps off the stairwell, the bun in her hair blocking the fake stained-glass moon in the window above our front door.

"Babe, what're you up to in here?"

"Just clearing stuff out, Ma. I've decided we have to start eating better."

She negotiates walking quickly into the kitchen, which you'd think would sound like a thunderstorm but is instead something even more ominous—the low groan of a boiler about to explode. That was the original ending of *The Shining*, by the way: In the novel, the boiler explodes and kills them all. Obviously vastly different from the movie. Spoiler alert.

"Quinny," Mom says, her forehead in a twist. "Why would you throw away all this good food?"

I pull a Cocoa Krispies box out of the Hefty bag and shake it. There is a delayed response from inside, the cereal *ca-chunk-ing* against the box like it's been awakened from the terrible reality of being, well, Cocoa Krispies.

"I don't know if we can call this food 'good,' Mama."

"But that was her favorite."

I lower the box. I stick my head into the Hefty. She's right. I've just completely disrupted the museum that was Annabeth's life. Shit.

"Well . . . maybe I could toss out some of the stuff she never touched?" I pick out a string cheese from the Hefty bag. Annabeth hated string cheese—even before it was flecked with green, like this one is now. "Like this?"

It starts with a quiver. Mom's breakdowns always start with a little quiver. Either chin or eyelid, and you really have to be artful about spotting it. She is a beautiful woman but also a large woman.

"I suppose," she says, but it's her chin this time. It's quivering.

I touch her on the shoulder. It's not okay. She's not ready for this.

"Go watch your stories," I say, "and I'll put everything back."

She looks away. She is embarrassed. She is *grieving*. Dammit, Quinn, don't embarrass your mom. You are smarter than this.

"Just for now," she says. "For now, I want everything back the way it was. I'm just not ready." She places her hand on the counter, right on top of that postcard advertising BOLD summer haircuts.

"I've gotta pee," I say, and I dash up the stairs. "I'll put all the food back in a sec!"

"I took the liberty of doing your whites while you were out!" Mom calls out, just as I'm discovering a stack of underwear outside my bedroom in the most perfect pile you've ever seen. I stare at it as if a baby has been delivered to my door.

"You went in my room?" I say. I didn't have to pee. I just had to get away.

"I'm tired of seeing you in that T-shirt," she says. "And I cleaned out some of the clutter, too."

I stomp my foot down once, hard. I'm mad and I don't know why. Why am I mad to see clean laundry? And then it hits me.

I throw my door open and skid across my floor, rug-burning my knee with something even worse, because I don't have a rug. Ignore. My lamp topples over, but I ignore that, too, frantic as I pull my desk out from the wall, to search beneath it.

It's there, streaked with sweat: the form for that student filmmakers' competition, which Mom never even knew we were thinking of applying to. The application feels like a bomb in my hand, ticking off all the things I was going to do but didn't, until *BOOM*.

See, in order for us to even apply to the competition, I would've had to *first* finish a full-length screenplay. That was the plan: I'd finish my screenplay, Annabeth would shoot a few scenes, and what the hell, we'd apply to this competition thing. If we'd gotten in, it would have meant a real mentor and, better yet, a couple of weeks away in LA this summer. Nothing sounds better than "away" right now.

Tick-tick-tick . . . BOOM.

I take the application across my room. I open my closet. I jump up and slide it on top of the teetering stack of textbooks I haven't touched since December twentieth.

"I'm happy to do your colors, too," Mom calls from downstairs.

My lips taste like contact lens solution, like salt and saline and oyster brine. I'm still mad but I'm also not. "Okay." I don't understand how somebody as skinny as me is supposed to keep all of these conflicting emotions inside without bursting a few seams.

Entire seasons have shifted since the last time I did a

proper load of laundry. I gather every last black sock and blue sweatshirt into my broken hamper and I walk them all down to the basement, where Mom is now leaning into the washing machine.

"Thanks," I say. I kiss her on the cheek. My mouth descends a full inch into her face, like when you haven't ridden your bike all year and the first time on you're like, *Dammit, Dad needs to fill up these tires.* Mom's cheeks have that kind of give to them.

It's adorable.

I go upstairs. I find my earplugs. And now I'm lying on my bed, wondering how Geoff and I could have been so incredibly intent on getting me a new AC today and then have completely forgotten to install it after the party tonight. How it's just sitting in the trunk of his brand-new Corolla while I broil.

The house shifts. Left to right. Left to right. Here she comes.

"Knock-knock," Mom says, standing outside the threshold of my room. I love how she's suddenly pretending to respect my privacy, even though she barged in here earlier and straightened my desk and did my whites and threw away my towering pizza box art. "I found something in the back pocket of your shorts."

"Oh." Earplugs: out. "You did?"

I am the least scandalous teen on earth, so I'm not sure

why I'm instantly nervous. What do I think Mom might have found? Not a condom. Not a cigarette. A nothing. I have the secret life of a retired librarian. All I do is read screenplays and watch movies. I don't even know if 7UP mixes with vodka, because I forgot to take a sip almost the moment I was handed the red cup tonight.

Mom makes her way across my room and hands me a tiny slip of paper.

"I lied, earlier," Mom says. Red flag. Mom never lies. "I said I did your laundry because I'm tired of seeing you in that T-shirt."

I cover myself up. I'm in my old robe, but it feels weird for Mom to see my bare legs on my bed, or something.

"Okay?" I go. "My feelings weren't hurt, don't worry. I'm tired of that shirt, too."

She waves away my words. "No, I mean—I saw that you went into Daddy's closet. You left it open after."

"Oh."

"And I won't have you wearing that man's clothes."

Just in case he comes back, by the way. She hates him, but mostly she hates him for leaving, and so we'd better not disturb his stuff. She hates him and she wants him back, and her daughter, too, while you're at it, God.

"Oh, yeah, of course, Mom. Yeah. I hate his clothes, too."

She attempts a smile. False start. "Maybe when we get the next grocery delivery, we can add some new cologne to the

order too. Because I won't have you *smelling* like him either."
And she flips around and attempts to make a quick, witty
exit.

When the last stairway step has stopped squeaking, I
unfold the slip of paper Mom gave me, and I hear a gasp. And
it's me who's gasping, and I taste humidity in the intake and I
gasp again.

It's just, I am so shocked by what I see that my writer
mind takes over, as if I'm watching the movie of my life from
overhead—a removed witness who still believes this screenplay has a chance of ending happily.

INT. QUINN'S BEDROOM - NIGHT

Quinn sits up straight on his twin bed. His
maroon robe falls open, but he doesn't adjust
it. He is too distracted.

We see his eyes widen as he stares at a slip of
paper in his hand.

Over his shoulder, we see it's the exact same
slip of paper on which the Celebrity name
"Mario Lemieux" had been written earlier
tonight -- only now, written above "Mario
Lemieux," in different handwriting, are the

words "I had no idea who," and underneath
"Mario Lemieux" is written: "was either."

                         QUINN
               Oh my freaking God.

We tilt down to see what Quinn sees: that
underneath "I had no idea who Mario Lemieux was
either" is a name, and a phone number.

The name is "Amir."

                                        CUT TO:

EXT. QUINN'S ROOF - NIGHT

Quinn dances around in the rain, his robe fully
open, his mouth filling with the holy water of
redemption.

Except, hello—no. Because you can't stand on our roof
without falling off. And it's not raining out.

Who cares, though? The first part of the scene is really happening. I couldn't have written it better. Amir doesn't know
who a legendary hockey player is either. Amir is not majoring
in Irony. Amir is not straight.

People: *This is what we know so far.*

```
INT. QUINN'S BEDROOM - NIGHT

Quinn paces, staring at the slip of paper and
giggling. But there is fear on his face too. Or
maybe just annoyance. . . .
```

Ugh. When Rory C. Lewis came out at school last year, the principal called a Diversity Assembly to honor him, which was the forty longest minutes of my *life*, and I'm including gym class in that tally. Rory gave a speech on the beauty and drama of being different, and got kind of an obligatory standing ovation.

But the truth is: Nobody ever made fun of Rory because he was gay, even before he was out, even though we could all tell he was gay. We didn't care that he was gay. We made fun of Rory because he is *annoying*.

I'm still not out. It just seems like such a hassle to *come* out. I want to just *be* out.

I look at the sheet of paper. My hands are making it flutter. I wonder how Amir got this into my back pocket. Maybe when I backed up into him at the sink. I wonder if Mom knows what this piece of paper means. Maybe . . . not, actually.

You know how older gay guys always say their "moms knew," when they finally came out to them. "I knew, I knew from the beginning," these Hollywood-sensitive moms always seem to be saying. That's not how it'll go with my mom. Sorry. She is as old-fashioned as you can get. She was "shocked" when she found out I was a friggin' *vegetarian*. She's been dropping hints about me marrying Tiffany Devlin, the six-toed girl across the street, since the day they moved in. I was *ten*.

I get off my bed. I am suddenly hungry for lunch meat. (I am not a vegetarian anymore.) But there's no lunch meat in my mini-fridge. Of course there isn't. All I've got is a six-pack of Sprite, saved for special occasions.

I look at Amir's handwriting again. It is so boyish and messy that I want to eat it.

In ten seconds I've torn everything off the corkboard above my desk, and when every last elementary school ribbon is fully cleared, I tack a pushpin through the "o" of Mario Lemieux.

But all I'm really looking at is Amir's phone number.

And then I celebrate. For once, I celebrate. I drink two Sprites, back to back, until I get the biggest and greatest stomachache ever and forever amen, and I don't even burp. I just hold it all in, and somehow my seams don't burst.

CHAPTER EIGHT

See, this is what I mean. Where's your dad when you need him to fill your bike's tires?

I'm in the garage after the most sleepless night in forever, starring sweat and boners. My old bike, covered in a veritable carpet of cobwebs, is straight out of an early-career Tim Burton movie. I hose it off and find our air pump, and after taking six minutes to figure out even *how* to fill up the tires, I mount the seat and bust out laughing. Man, this thing is set for a different Quinn. A younger one. A shorter one. The one who was a brother.

I adjust the seat and then I duck my head inside the house and go, "I'll see you later, Mom. I'm off to solve the case of who broke into my room last night and made my clothes clean," and I'm saying it in my uptight-detective voice that always makes her giggle, and so when the door shuts behind me and

I hear Mom's laughter fill the sunroom, that feels really great.

Five minutes down Morrow Road, a car from behind gives me this quick *honk-honk*, and I'm not sure if it's a "sorry about your sister" honk or a "nice haircut, homo" honk or a "hey, you're riding in the middle of the road and you're going really slow" honk—but all three of those things are entirely possible, and so I pull over where the road forks and take a breath.

Is today the day to make a right, and coast by the school, and see the mural of my big sister looking like a big pug?

I lift my tires from the grass and face them left. Another day. And just before I take off again to find Geoff at Loco Mocha and get an iced something—because, oh my God, an iced anything will be delicious today, the first nutrition I've actually earned in, oh, half a year—I spot a firefly on a daisy.

"Hello, little firefly," I say. "You're not supposed to be outside in the daytime."

Basically it is unbelievable how sweet I can be when nobody is watching.

EXT. HILL OUTSIDE QUINN'S NEIGHBORHOOD - DAY

Quinn wipes the sweat from his neck and kneels down to press his finger to a daisy. The firefly looks at him and smiles.

                    FIREFLY
          Are you my friend?

Quinn is startled to hear the firefly speak --
especially since he generally hates animated
films.

                    QUINN
          Sure, if you're willing to have
          a male friend named "Quinn."

The firefly laughs. Her butt lights up.

                    FIREFLY
          You're funny.

                    QUINN
          I am?

                    FIREFLY
          You are.

                    QUINN
          That's nice. It's been a while
          since anyone's said that.

The firefly steps onto Quinn's finger. It's
been a long time since anything has trusted him
like this.

I wipe the sweat from my neck and kneel over. For two seconds I allow myself the possibility that the firefly might actually speak to me.

But when I press my finger to the flower, she just flies away.

"Hey, do you carry helmets?"

"Aisle six."

I'm working on a new theory. The new theory is that every
person gets corrupted at some point. That there is *a moment*
that changes you forever, from this to that. Innocent to wary.

Example: Tiffany Devlin, across the street, was born with
six toes on her left foot, and one day in the fourth grade she
arrived as "the new girl" in school, and we all just instantly
nicknamed her Toe-fanny, like it was *Lord of the Flies*. Now, it
was not particularly original, as slurs go—this is coming from
"Queen" Roberts—but you get the drift. You don't want to be
called Toe-fanny if you're a kid with six toes.

That day was Tiffany's corruption. Welcome to the neighborhood.

I bend over in this sports equipment place and hunt for the
cheapest helmet. There are so many options here that I feel like
I'm shopping for air conditioners again.

Anyway, the minute you get corrupted is the moment you understand what it feels like to lose something. Not when you lose a Little League game. Not when you lose a grandparent, even. That's not a scandal—that's nature. What's everybody doing crying over their eighty-five-year-old Nana dropping dead in her nursing home in the middle of crafts day? What did you *think* was going to happen? That Nana was going to be the first person *literally ever* who bucked the trend known as the Life Cycle? Not a scandal. Roll the credits.

I walk this seventeen-dollar jet-black helmet to the cash register up front. See, I'm buying it because after the firefly flew away, I got back on my bike and this car whipped around the fork blasting country music (always trouble), and it nearly killed me flat. Like: I felt the hair on my face (I don't really have to shave yet; it's like a step up from peach fuzz) get literally *grazed*.

Now that I know what it's like to lose something real—December twentieth was my corruption—everything is different. You start doing stuff like buying yourself helmets, even if you're only sixteen. You start thinking: *Maybe I ought to remember to buckle up right away from now on.* It's not that I particularly know what I'm living for anymore. I'm an extremely limited filmmaker without the vision and silent encouragement of my sister—the only person I ever read my first drafts out loud to. I just can't stand the thought of Mom losing both her kids in a single year.

I mean, really. I love a good *Terms of Endearment* as much as the next guy, but not as my fucking life.

● ● ●

Geoff is working the coffee counter. I get in line and start to get really giggly that he hasn't noticed me yet. He's going to flip. He's got the branded Loco Mocha hat on and everything. He looks cute, for Geoff. Something's off, though.

"Quinn!" He spots me, finally, and flashes the goony grin. "How did you get here?"

"Your dad gave me a free Corolla."

"Wait, what?"

"I'm kidding."

Geoff comes out from behind the counter and gives me one of those straight-boy half hugs. I realize what's off now. His mustache. Literally. Thank God.

"Jesus, you could have warned me," he says, pulling away.

"Sorry." My body is now where sweat goes to party.

"Can I get your order started?" he asks. He is so psyched, and runs back around behind the glass case.

"Yes, which size iced coffee is big enough for me to bathe in?"

This girl behind the counter kind of glares at Geoff. He nervous-laughs.

"Do you want a Caffeine Level Four?" he says. (There are four sizes at Loco Mocha. Even the Level One has enough jolt to fuel an overnight study binge.)

"Make it a Two."

"Will the following guest *please* step *down*?" the girl says, and she scoots Geoff out of her way with her hip. He gives me the sorry grin.

"When's your next break?" I ask him.

The girl rolls her eyes and doesn't even look at Geoff. "You can take a five now, but you have to come back early from lunch."

"Cool." He whips off his hat like it's a costume, and we walk to two large leather chairs across the store and plop down. The chair cushions hiss and wheeze and kind of burp, which makes us laugh, because we're secretly still thirteen years old.

"You still have my AC," I go.

"Yes," he says, "I know. I literally got to the end of your street last night and pulled over and texted you a hundred times, but, you know—if you never turn your phone on, you can't receive messages."

I'm not turning the phone on again. "I'm anti-cell these days." Nobody but the police and my therapist know why. Thank God it didn't get out to the local press. I can barely live with myself as it is, with*out* people knowing the full story.

"You are literally worse with technology than my Nana. My *Nana* sends me GIFs, Quinn. My Nana."

I thought his Nana dropped dead during crafts day last year. I've gotta stop rewriting other people's lives.

"You should stick around for my lunch break," he says. "We'll pop over to the Verizon store. It's time to get a new phone."

I wave him away. "You could have just walked right back through our front door last night. That never stopped you before. I *needed* that air conditioner."

Geoff is using his finger to doodle something invisible into the arm of his chair. His autograph, I think. He wants to be famous; he just doesn't know what for, yet. I love him for this.

"I didn't want to freak out your mom," Geoff says. "The porch light was off."

Boring scene. Change the stakes: "So, something *happened* last night," I say to him. My heart plays hopscotch, and it isn't just the caffeine.

This moment is the reason for the entire bike excursion, but here's another theory: When you've got big news, don't even *think* about how you'll write it or you'll choke. Same goes for standardized tests, by the way.

"Geoff," the girl calls over, cocking an eyebrow from behind the counter. A line is forming.

"Okay, what?" he says to me. "Be quick."

Perfect. That's all I want this to be. But I feel my face close in on itself, like Mom's does when she doesn't get my humor. I'm not confused, though, just unsure about how to deliver this. Is this a comic scene? Where does this occur in the screenplay of my life, and is Geoff's character going to be weirded out?

I'm in my head. Dammit. Don't write, Quinn, just talk.

"Dude," he says, but in a sweet way.

I look around to make sure we're not being overheard. Some terrible jazz music plays overhead, and when the horns get loud, I get quiet.

"You know when we were little," I say, "and I used to put your sister's ballet tutus on my head, before we knew it was kind of strange for boys to do that?"

Geoff puts his palm up to my face and stands. "Quinn, is this about you being gay? I literally don't care at all."

Um, what? "Um." He knows? Wait, Geoff knows. Wait, did somebody tell him? Wait, I've never told *anyone*.

"I have to get back to work," he says. "Can we not make a big deal out of this? Unless, I mean, you want to."

"*Geoff*, for *real*," the girl goes. But I realize she's not a girl. She's a manager. She's still training Geoff.

"One sec, Venessa. This is important."

"I mean," I go, hoping the song will get even louder. Bring on the cymbals. "I'm not sure if I'm gay or what. I might be bi."

Geoff snort-laughs and punches my shoulder. "Yeah," he says, "and I might be European."

I don't totally know what this means, other than: Geoff is not European.

He puts his hat back on. "Quinn, I've known for, like, ever. Unless you're confessing that you're in love with me—" He stops. His face goes a little white. "Oh God, I mean—if you are, I'd be flattered, but—"

"Ew, Geoff. Please. You name your farts. Seriously."

We laugh. We laugh hard. He heads back to the counter, just as his manager gets a call on her cell. When she crouches behind the seasonal drink display in order to take it, she thinks that nobody's watching her, but I am. I see everything. It's haunting. It is not a gift to see everything, believe me.

"Okay, I guess I'm . . . heading home, then," I say. Turns out this is a very minor scene. Might even end up on the cutting-room floor. I like that.

"No," Geoff goes, after he rings up another customer, "you're getting a *phone* at the Verizon store and then you're texting me which foreign film we're seeing tonight."

I hate foreign films. "Who said I want to see a foreign film tonight?" I don't want to have to *read* at a movie.

"My bad," Geoff says, resting his elbows on the counter. "I thought all gay dudes were, like, obsessed with foreign films." He is teasing.

"Geoff, keep your voice down." I look around again. *"Relax."*

"You relax, you big queen," he says. I gasp again. He is totally poking fun at me. He is totally the best.

I turn to the parking lot, shaky, but then: "Hey," I say, back to Geoff, "what happened to your mustache?"

Okay, imagine the theme music to *Jaws*, because his manager is BACK. She takes a rag and wipes down the counter, and when she sees that Geoff isn't busy, she literally puts his hand on the rag to take over, and *then* she looks at me like I'm in her living room ruining Christmas morning.

"The *mustache*," the manager says—to *me*!—"wasn't professional-looking."

Geoff gently puts his head against the refrigerated food case and closes his eyes like he's really embarrassed. I take a step toward him. He looks up. The manager turns to the next customer. Geoff winks at me.

"See you later—girlfriend," he says.

"Geoff. I'll kill you."

But there we go again. Laughing.

I pivot away, and hold the icy cup up to my neck in preparation for the smack of heat outside. But just before I'm out the door, Geoff goes "Psst!" like we're seven years old, making a couch-cushion fort in his basement. Back when our parents were friends and our big sisters took ballet together and we weren't gay or straight, we were just Quinny and Geoffy.

"Yeah?" I say.

"Amir Turani," Geoff says, louder than Annabeth would have directed him to speak, "thinks you have a cute butt."

CHAPTER NINE

I'm late for Staring Practice.

"Like I said," my therapist goes, adjusting her laptop screen and giving me a nostril view that one could describe as "vivid." "We can use your remaining time however you'd like, Quinn."

We're thirty minutes into our regular forty-five-minute Skype session, but we're really just three minutes into it; see, it wasn't till Geoff and I had taken seats in the almost sadistically powerful air-conditioning of his Corolla and each had a foot-long hoagie (I waited for his lunch break) that I even realized I was missing the only Thursday therapy session I've ever actually wanted to have.

You've never seen a guy pedal home so fast. Sparks flew from my wheels, at least in my mind.

"I've just got a ton to figure out today," I say, still willing my heart to slow down.

"Start from the beginning, then."

I can barely concentrate, though, because hovering just above my laptop screen is Amir's handwriting on the slip of Celebrity paper.

Incoming boner.

"I met a guy," I say, in a quiet way. "At this party."

My therapist barely conceals a smile. "I *see*." She stares, and stares. Dammit. She has picked up on my techniques and mastered them.

"Am I allowed to, like, talk about sex stuff with you?" Gah. I want to slam my computer screen shut. My therapist is the stepmom of this second-tier boy at school. She sees me for a "deeply discounted" rate because her son was friends with Annabeth, and they feel bad for us.

"Of course you can talk about sex stuff," she says. "For many people, that's all they talk about."

Wow. "Okay," I say. I look out my window. No lemonade stand in sight. "So this college guy said I have a nice butt." Gah. I can't believe I'm saying this to a, like, mom-lady. "I mean, he didn't say it to me—he said it through friends. That I have an okay butt or whatever. Through Geoff's sister."

"I see," my therapist says, and I take over staring duties to make her talk. It works. "People have long noticed you for your looks, Quinn, but now one *particular* boy has. How are you feeling about that?" I lower the volume on my computer. Mom is snoozing in the sunroom, but suddenly I develop a theory that the air vents in our house deliver sound better than I've made note of recently, since I'm so frequently in earplugs.

"Well, I don't know how to communicate with him," I say.

"Most people start with honesty." She laughs—a therapist joke, I guess. Hard to tell. Her side of the screen is always blurry because I truly believe people over the age of fifty aren't willing to splurge for good Internet. "Okay, that's not always true," she says. I have her pegged at fifty-three, by the way. "But it's *best* to start with honesty. I advocate for honesty."

"No," I say, talking faster than I mean to. "I mean: I literally don't know how to get *ahold* of him."

"Might this be the time to finally power your phone back up? Would you like to turn it on during this session? Together?"

No way. "I'm not even sure where it is, to be honest. It's somewhere here, but I don't know where. But I'm *not ready*." I say that part loud, because he who's loudest wins, at least according to Dad.

So, scratch that theory, actually.

"All right, then," my therapist says. I don't remember about what.

"The problem is, I have this amazing idea," I say. "I kind of want to ask Amir out, but not like on a date, but like on a group situation, I mean."

"Could you send out an e-mail?"

I wave my hands. "I hate e-mail. Nobody checks e-mail."

She begins playing almost flirtily with her silk scarf. That's a first. "Go old-fashioned, then," she says. "It's very Quinn Roberts to buck trends. Ask him out through Geoff. That could be charming to an older man."

I chuckle. "'An older man,' that's hilarious. Amir's only, like, nineteen, I bet."

"The difference between a sixteen-year-old and a nineteen-year-old can be substantial, Quinn," she says, even though I'm seventeen this Sunday. "But I'll leave that for you to discover."

Great. Now my stomach is a wooden roller coaster going off the rails. I don't want to discover anything. I want to just write it exactly the way I'd like it to play out onscreen.

"Unfortunately, our time today is up," she says. "But when you have a chance, I really do need you to ask your mom to open the mail sometime soon. We're now about three months behind on payment, and at some point—"

"Totally clear," I say. "I'll mention it to her today. See? I'm making a note of it right now."

I jiggle my arm just enough in the camera's frame so that it looks as if I'm writing something down on my desk. But I'm not. What I'm mainly doing is I'm thinking, *Thank God Mom's disability checks just get deposited straight to her bank account.*

"Thank you," my therapist says.

Her buzzer goes off, and she winces. This makes me happy. I have entertained her.

She likes me.

"Quinn, I have to get that," she says.

"Of course."

I'm already opening another tab on my screen, anyway: this torrent site to rip a few movies to binge on tonight.

"But I wanted to say something," she says.

"Uh-huh."

I consider downloading *The Philadelphia Story*. Maybe I could study Cary Grant and actually, you know, learn something about romance. I've never tried to woo a guy before. The closest I've come is that I once poured chocolate milk over Tommy "the Tank" Foster's mashed potatoes, in third grade.

LIFE HACK: Never pour chocolate milk over the mashed potatoes of anyone nicknamed "the Tank."

"Quinn, I'm logging off now, but—"

"Great, so, next Thursday."

"—did you hear what I just said? A moment ago."

"Oh." Shit. Minimize screen. Click back to Skype. Blink. "Sorry."

"It's okay," my therapist says. "But I said something important."

Jesus, maybe that school counselor of mine was right. Maybe multitasking *is* a dangerous myth.

"Okay?" I say.

"I said I'm proud of you."

It's so quiet in my room that I think I can hear Mom

snoring downstairs. Our vents really are connected. I knew it.

"For what?" I say. My therapist has never been proud of me.

"I shouldn't really say this," she says, "but—this is our first session in which you didn't mention your sister."

CHAPTER TEN

When I was ten years old, a new family moved in across the street. It caused a stir. Most people don't move *to* Pittsburgh.

Tiffany Devlin was my age, but I was immediately more interested in her substantially older brother. He was tall, and *nice*. At ten years old, *nice* wasn't the first adjective I'd have used to describe grown-up men. *Loud*, maybe. Or *sad*. But not *nice*.

Tiffany's twenty-two-year-old brother, Ricky Devlin—Tiffany was a "wonderful surprise," I remember her mom saying once to my mom—had helped his family move in, but he was only staying for the summer. "Just the summer."

"Why?" I asked Ricky once, weeks later, when he was babysitting me and Tiffany and Annabeth. "Why would you move in with your parents?" This boggled my mind—willingly living with your mom and dad, once you don't have to anymore.

"Well, I'm a screenwriter," he said.

"Don't movie people live in Hollywood?" Annabeth said, because Annabeth intuitively knew everything. Always.

"The ones who sell screenplays do," Ricky said, and that answered that. Something about it wasn't pathetic though. Ricky was golden, perfect.

He stayed in the Devlins' attic, and when it would get really hot, he'd put an oscillating fan in the center of the floor and hold a stick of deodorant up to it to give the room a "clean scent." Which apparently really stuck with me, ha. Ricky had a photo of the Hollywood sign taped to the sloped wall. He drank a lot of green juices and was always smiling, and he was never loud and never sad.

I wouldn't have consciously known Ricky was gay, but he must have been. *Please*, he ate raw almonds before it was trendy to, he didn't have a beer gut, and when he cried at the end of *The Shawshank Redemption*, he didn't wipe away his tears. I was embarrassed for him, and then I wasn't.

I fell in love with movies that summer.

I mean, if Ricky had been in love with dentistry, I'd have a whole other story. Maybe I wouldn't even see my life *as* a story at all, but I do. Ricky showed me how.

We started by screening the basics, something I'd never done with Dad. Classic films like *Old Yeller*. Man, how I bawled at that one. I guess I used to let people see me cry. While Annabeth and Tiffany were busy downstairs playing "fashion runway" or "house" or whatever, Ricky and I would go to the attic and watch like ten movies a weekend.

Nothing about it was creepy, so get your mind outta the gutter.

He taught me about this mythic story structure that a lot of screenwriters use. I was comforted by the idea of a time-tested way of telling a satisfying tale—because that was the summer when Mom and Dad started openly fighting, and when Annabeth became obsessed with "achievement" as a general concept, and when my A.D.D. began showing up in all sorts of mysterious and charming ways. That was the summer, I mean, when I started to not like the way my life story was going.

But if I used Ricky's time-tested method to plan out my plots, I'd always be able to find my way back home again.

Ricky printed out his version of the Hero's Journey for me once, and from then on out, whenever we'd hit a mythic story beat in a movie we were watching, he'd pause it and go, "See! That's the hero 'deciding to go.' That's the hero's journey, Quinny."

He made me promise to keep it safe.

RICKY DEVLIN'S HERO'S JOURNEY

We meet the hero in his ordinary world (at home, at
    school, etc.).

Hero gets called to action (aka the inciting incident).

Hero refuses the call to adventure (stays at home,
    makes excuses, plays video games instead, etc.).

Hero decides to go because: whatever.

Hero gets into a ton of trouble, but also has adventures and meets allies.

Shit happens.

Worse shit happens.

The worst shit happens and the hero's life is basically over.

But then the hero thinks of something amazing to break into the third act of the screenplay.

And he does.

And he learns something vital and true that he didn't even know was possible.

And he goes home smarter, if a little beaten up.

And I'm using "he" generally, but obviously a hero can be a she.

And if it's written really well and comes in under 110 pages, the screenwriter gets a house in the Hollywood Hills with a small pool. ☺

"So does *everybody* have a pool in Hollywood?" I became enamored of the idea of having my own little pool. I was going to make it in the shape of a *Q,* and the slash at the bottom of the *Q* was going to be the hot tub.

"Not everybody," Ricky said. "Only people who sell screenplays."

And so I started making up little scripts for movies, basically because I wanted a hot tub, ha. "These are good," Ricky said. He'd shown me how to format them on Mom's clunky old laptop, from the days when she worked for Alcoa, before she got injured and the disability checks starting rolling in. "But you need somebody to film them for you!" Ricky said. "Otherwise it's just words, and not a movie."

He wouldn't help me film the movies, himself. He was busy "re-revising" his screenplay—which was about this family whose house accidentally burns to the ground, and when it does, they discover a secret chamber in the basement that leads to an entirely other world where there's no such thing as fire. (Working title: *No Such Thing As Fire.*)

At the time I thought it was the best idea since, oh, *Star Wars.* I was Ricky's first fangirl.

"Get your big sister to shoot your little screenplays," he suggested. "You guys can be a pint-size moviemaking team, like the Coen Brothers."

That did it. I had found my "call to adventure." I had bypassed "the refusal." Hell, I was already on step four of my hero's journey; I loved the Coen Brothers, so that was all he had to say. Basically, when I was ten, I was obsessed with anything that had the f-word in it.

Annabeth always had better phones than I did; she was older. So that's how it started. She had a pretty good camera phone. And we had these endless summers—the kind of summers where you almost *want* school to start back up again— because we were the only kids whose parents didn't pay for camp at the Y. We just had us and our imaginations and a house with spotty air-conditioning.

My sister doesn't do anything half assed, so she went to the library and got out books on how to edit movies, and she started making me read my ten-page screenplays out loud to her, and only her. (After Annabeth and I teamed up, I never let anyone else see my first drafts. Too exposed. You can't trust most people.)

Then we went back to school that fall, and Annabeth started developing these bumps en route to boobs, and Ricky went away to Hollywood, became somebody, and never looked back. And never *came* back.

Somehow, he's still that golden guy to me, though, even now. The one who'd still bail me out today, if I really needed it.

Annabeth kept adding other skills to her repertoire that year, but not me. I'm not a particularly original thinker, I'm not, but I loved the order and formula and maybe even the safety of a script, with its margins and standards. So I stuck with it.

I just hate actually *filming* stuff, because immediately my vision gets crushed. You want a scene to take place on the sunniest, most beautiful day of the year, and suddenly a cloud passes over. Vision ruined.

So we'd get my miniscreenplays where we'd want them and I'd hand them off to Annabeth, and in her spare time she'd cast it and shoot it and edit it, and I'd see the final product and judge it and hate it and criticize it. But secretly I also loved it, because those were my words! People were saying my words!

Eventually, years into the whole thing, we even had an official company name: Q & A Productions. Nice, right? A fourth-tier art nerd at school even designed a pretty slick logo for us, and that was my identity: the silver *Q* of Q & A. You know, when *A* wasn't at Model U.N. or French Club or pep squad, or studying, or doing the hundred other things she seemed to get lost in, nearly as much as making our movies.

Anyway, you know what's a really stupid name? Q Productions. Just that. Because what is a *Q* without an *A*?

That's actually the most confusing part about being alive without knowing the end of your own hero's journey. You never know if it's time to go home or head into battle. You never know if you've already faced your biggest monster.

CHAPTER ELEVEN

My three newest-looking T-shirts are spread out on my bed as if they're the finalists in a very low-stakes fashion competition. To give you a sense of my definition of "newest": One of them has a hole in it in the shape of Florida. Regardless: New day, new me, ta-da.

"Not to be a mom," Mom says, "but *please* be careful on the wooden roller coasters today. I don't trust them at all."

Now I'm in the kitchen, downing a glass of water. A root beer would be so delicious right now, but this is not the day to be a burp monster.

"Of course, Mom. I'll avoid the wooden coasters entirely."

Bald-faced lie. I chose Kennywood for my first group date with Amir so that if it goes terribly, I'll at least have the chance of making the news: YOUNGER BROTHER OF GIFTED GIRL THROWN FROM BACKSEAT OF JACK RABBIT. CLICK FOR VIDEO.

"I'm gonna wait outside, Ma."

She rocks herself up from the wicker lounger. "Give Geoffrey my best."

"Will do, Ma! And guess what?"—I'm already halfway out the door—"He shaved off the mustache, just for you!"

Slam.

It's a pitiful kind of poverty when, in the middle of a June heat wave, the pavement outside your house is cooler than your mattress is upstairs. We really *have* to get that AC installed. And maybe I really *should* get a job. I walk the square lines of cement, toe to heel, creating a dumb little game with childish rules (walk three steps, hop once) that may as well be called: "How to avoid thinking about making conversation with a guy who's in college."

Well, there you go. I picture Amir Turani on the big screen of my brain and here goes my imagination.

EXT. PAVEMENT OUTSIDE QUINN'S HOUSE - DAY

Quinn, looking casually stylish in a solid
red T-shirt layered on top of a faded black
one with a hole in the shape of Florida, leans
against his mom's mailbox.

At the top of the big hill leading down to his

small house, a pair of headlights cut through the broiling waves rising off summer asphalt. Quinn perks up but plays it cool.

So cool his upper lip isn't even sweating.

A BLUE MINIVAN pulls up. It's blasting the song of the summer. Perfect. Quinn knows this one.

Geoff rolls down the window from the front passenger seat; CARLY is driving.

                    GEOFF
          Hop in!

Quinn opens the sliding minivan door. His eyebrows crinkle: *Where's Amir?* And then, as if he's reading Quinn's mind:

                    AMIR
          Back here.

Quinn cranes his neck to spy into the van's backseat. Smile.

                    GEOFF

          Let's *go*! There's a corn dog
          with your name on it waiting
          for you at the greatest
          amusement park in Western
          Pennsylvania.

Quinn rolls his eyes at Amir, and the two
share a laugh the way a young couple might have
shared a milk shake in the fifties.

As Quinn gets in, the song switches over to
something he doesn't recognize -- we see him
get a bit panicked -- but Amir covers for him.

                    AMIR

          So, you've been to Kennyland
          before?

Quinn giggles, but in a way that's sweet and
also masculine.

                    QUINN

          Kenny*wood*, yes. I practically
          grew up there. I know all the
          best rides, all the cleanest

bathrooms, all the least-gross
foods. You know, if you're
into that sort of thing.

                    AMIR
        I'm into that sort of thing.
        Though I get a little scared
        on roller coasters.

                    QUINN
        Good to know.

Carly pulls onto the parkway, cranking up the
music.

                    AMIR
        So, like, you'll protect me?

                    QUINN
        Duh.

                                CUT TO:

EXT. KENNYWOOD AMUSEMENT PARK - LATER

Quinn stumbles off a roller coaster, his face
green, his eyes crossed. Amir couldn't be

having a better time, but Quinn can barely
handle the intensity of these rides. He's not a
kid anymore. He looks like he's gonna hurl.

Carly and Geoff pop into respective bathrooms,
leaving Quinn and Amir alone by a cotton candy
vendor.

> AMIR

Should we take a break?

> QUINN

Nah. That's okay.

Amir takes Quinn's hand. A first.

> AMIR

You sure?

> QUINN

Uh . . . I *could* be persuaded
to find a bench and have a
Coke. . . .

Amir smiles and pulls Quinn under the awning of
a corn dog hut. They look up at a menu.

<pre>
                    AMIR

        Pepsi okay?

                    QUINN

                 (sweetly)

        Never.

Quinn leans in to kiss—
</pre>

Honk. *Honnnk.*

For some reason, I've got the neck band of one of my T-shirts in my mouth, and this is the moment—with a wet collar and stubbly hair that is probably already shiny with unconfident summer sweat—that a car pulls up to my mom's mailbox. Not a blue minivan, though—there never was a blue minivan in my world to begin with, only in my screenplay vision of this moment—but rather a beat-up silver Saturn. It looks like it hasn't been washed since, oh, the Gold Rush.

"Get in," Geoff says from the front passenger seat. I squint. Carly isn't driving; Amir is. Carly's in the backseat. Why is *Carly* in the backseat?

Annabeth would know how to storyboard this sequence.

"Well, get *in*, babe," I hear. Mom's behind us on our front stoop, making a rare appearance outside. "Geoffrey's been laying on the horn for twenty seconds!"

I reach for the hot-hot handle of Amir's Saturn, and when

it won't budge, he calls out the window: "Oh, sorry, that door is busted. Get in on Carly's side."

Okay, then. "Not a problem!" I say, *way* too agreeably, as if anyone would have a problem with this. Idiot.

"See you later, Mrs. R.!" Geoff shouts, and I slide onto Carly's side into a car that's whirring with air-conditioning, and something that sounds different from the song of the summer: the sound of anticipation.

Carly hands me a pair of eyeglasses: thick-rimmed, 1960s spectacles that look like something Gary Busey would have worn in *The Buddy Holly Story*. (1978 semiclassic. You can skip it.)

I give Carly a "What the hell?" look, but she just stares unblinkingly at me until I slide them on. They don't have a prescription. They are fashion glasses. Carly is decorating me for my date.

"Buckle *up*," she goes.

"Roller coasters, here we come," I say back, and then nobody else adds much of anything for the rest of the ride. But the song of the summer comes on twice—that happens—and at least I recognize it, almost like I'm a first-tier boy who knows what's what.

CHAPTER TWELVE

Kennywood amusement park is one of only two in the country that are registered as National Historic Landmarks, which is to say: These rides are old as fuck. And made out of wood. When was the last time anything wooden lasted a long time, other than trees? Wood *breaks* and *splinters* in the weather. And Pittsburgh has a lot of weather.

That makes the Jack Rabbit especially dangerous, because it's not just a wooden roller coaster but also one that has a famous double dip that nearly throws people from the last row. Mom never let us ride in the last row.

"Remember the rumor in third grade that a student from West Mifflin was thrown from the last row?" Geoff says when he and I pull down the safety bar—in the last row. Amir and Carly are riding in front of us, which is good by me. Can't come on too strong too early. Also, I caught Amir checking out my butt in the ticket line, so my confidence is good for at least twenty minutes, ha.

"Have you ever been on a wooden roller coaster?" I try to shout up to him, but the wind and the general clanking kind of drown out my voice, and I'm immediately glad for this, because what kind of an idiot tries to flirt on a roller coaster with somebody in a different row. (ANSWER: the last American virgin, that kind of idiot.)

We hit the one stride of smooth coasting on the Rabbit, and Geoff points to where glasses would sit on his face, if he wore them.

"Looks good," he mouths, just as we hit the infamous double dip and both of us throw our arms in the air. Laughter. But also fear. I grab the bar with a psycho grip. A first. My eyes are squeezed closed now. I wish I had my new helmet on.

"Jeez, Louise," Geoff says, which he always says when I act like a big girl. (I'm a feminist, by the way, so no offense!)

We pull back into the station and Amir whips his head around and goes: "Well, that was something."

"You ain't seen nothing yet," I say, convincingly enough, and we all lift our lap bars and try to walk in a straight line out of the station—but the thing about wooden coasters is: They will screw up your equilibrium and make you all unsure on your feet, which is (theory alert) secretly why we love them so much; there's nothing better than not quite feeling like yourself. I mean, at least if you're me.

"Potato Patch?" Carly says, and Geoff flicks her arm and goes, "Calm down, carb hoarder. It's like eleven a.m."

"Okay," I say, "we're going on the Racer, next, now."

"Whoa-ho-ho, pulling out all the big guns," Geoff goes. He's right. The Racer is in my top three rides at Kennywood.

"So, *le* next roller coaster, *s'il vous plaît*?" Amir says in this goofy French accent, and I lead the way with what can only be described as a bounce in my step. LIFE HACK: Memorize anything, from amusement park shortcuts to how to make a decent plate of spaghetti, and you, too, can appear to be an expert about something for a good four hours. It's always the fifth hour when things get tricky.

"Get ready to have your ass whooped," Geoff says to Amir, pausing as our group parts around some pretty adorable toddlers all tied together by their wrists and drooling en masse.

"Um," Amir says.

"Geoff sucks at context and setup," I say, jumping in as we pass a frozen lemonade stand, and getting an odd boner. "What he means to say is: The Racer is another wooden coaster, but there's two tracks on this one, side by side. And one group is in one train and the other is in the, like, other, and it's totally random which train is going to win." I pause. "And my car has never lost, like, ever."

Keep it shorter, Quinn. Nail the punch lines today and let Geoff do the speeches.

"Two roller-coaster cars *race* each other," Carly says to

Amir, as if this clarifies anything. She's wearing these extremely uncomfortable-looking gladiator boot-sandals.

"I think I get the concept," Amir says. "I had this stepuncle who raced cars."

"Oh, no way," I say, as if this is a clever catchphrase, which it's not.

"Way," he goes.

His outfit today, by the way: Literally who cares. You should see his hair. It is a little too long and it is so moppy and cute.

We get in the back of the Racer line, and suddenly the fact that we're not walking makes me antsy. I'm pretty good at making nervous conversation when there are other senses being occupied, but standing and talking while making eye contact always feels so formal to me, like we're parents on the edge of a playground when the truth is we're still kids ourselves.

"So, where are you from, Amir?" Geoff finally goes.

"Dallas," Amir says. "But I'm not actually *from* there. I grew up all over. Basically anywhere that an Iranian-American gay kid wouldn't feel comfortable."

Silence. Geoff's looking at me and goes, "Like, *where* else?"

Always dangerous when a straight boy has to feed *you* the dialogue. But see, what I'm wanting to do is just list every movie ever shot in Dallas. There are some classics. . . .

"Maryland . . . Virginia," Amir says, "a bunch of one-traffic-light towns."

"Cool," Geoff goes.

"Trivia," I say, suddenly and with finality. This is a game I play with Geoff in which I say "Trivia" and he groans because he never knows a-n-y of my trivia.

We move up in line.

"Trivia?" Amir goes. Geoff is groaning. Called it.

"Name a film that was primarily shot in both Dallas and Pittsburgh," I say.

Carly is giving me the exact look she gave me after I told her I wet one of her sleeping bags (when I was seven, relax).

"Okay," Amir goes, playing along because he's wonderful, "is it a movie that obviously takes place in either Dallas or Pittsburgh?"

"Good question," I'm starting to say, when Geoff jumps in and goes, "*Wrong*, you're not allowed to ask questions in Trivia." I could kill him. Carly whaps him upside the head and goes, "Don't act like yourself today, G-force."

"I'm breaking all the rules," Amir says, pinching the fabric of his salmon-pink shorts. "Parking on the wrong side of the lot, asking questions during Quinn's famous games. . . ."

Is this flirting? If this isn't flirting, this is what flirting should be redefined as. What could this master flirter even *see* in me?

"No," I say, "this film does not take place in either Dallas or Pittsburgh." I look at Geoff. "Excellent question. New rule: You're allowed to ask questions during Trivia as long as they're intelligible. Geoff, this rules you out."

Carly giggles but Amir doesn't, and I picture how sweet he was during Celebrity and suddenly wonder if I'm too big of a jagoff for him. Isn't everybody from Texas warm spirited and polite? You have to work really hard to be polite when you're me—the son of a categorically large woman—because the glares that people used to give her, when she'd leave our house, would turn even the biggest saint in Pittsburgh ice hearted. Even in this heat.

"Man, it's hot," Carly says. We're almost at the front of the line. A nearby rando has just won a dirty-looking teddy bear, and the guy's girlfriend is toting the thing around with a degree of pride non-Pittsburghers would typically reserve for finishing a medical degree a year early.

"Can you give us another clue?" Amir says.

"Okay," I say, looking away because his eyes are so pretty, "the main special effect that the film is known for was created by the same guy who masterminded John Carpenter's *The Thing*."

You can practically hear the three of them blinking, but still, Amir smiles. I'll describe his smile to you: perfect.

"Wow," he goes, "okay. . . ."

Dammit, I'm losing him.

"Oh!" I say, thumping my hand on a garbage can lid that is so immediately scalding that I pull it away but act as if nothing has happened. "The film was originally rated X."

"X?" Geoff says.

"That's, like, vintage NC-17," Amir says, which is nice. We're finally up to the front, one ride away from racing. "Usually for graphic sex."

The phrase *graphic sex* should give me another boner, but it doesn't, not at all. The phrase *graphic sex* just reminds me I don't yet know how to have even ungraphic sex. There isn't a scene from the screenplay of my life so far that would even get flagged as PG-13.

We're up. Thank God.

"Okay, pick your cars," says the kid manning the Racer. When we were little, the employees here seemed *so* old. . . .

"Go with Quinny, Amir," Carly says. "His car always wins."

Bless her.

And so we climb in, and just as the train is pulling out of the station, Amir goes:

"Okay, one more clue and then I give up."

"It was shot in the eighties," I say, "it's about robots and, like, crime; it won the Oscar for sound. . . . I mean, if I give you any more clues, I'm just going to have to say—"

The Racer rings its signature starting bell, its brakes hiss off, and Amir and I lock eyes and go, "*RoboCop*," with identical intonations and delivery and timing, and we bust into howls as our red car cranks around the first bend and *click-click-clicks* up the first mini-incline. Here we go.

"Yes," I say, "*RoboCop* for the gold." As if I've ever given out medals during Trivia. All new rules today.

Geoff and I catch sight of each other from across the tracks, something we've done on this ride for more than a decade, and I wait for him to do the mock-competitive fist-punch he always does, but instead he does this big cheesy smile like I've come back from the dead for one night only.

"Oh, gosh," I hear Amir say, not in a way that's cinematic at all but rather small and novelistic. That's when I realize he's pressing the full weight of his knee into mine, and that I can feel his soft leg hair Velcro-ing into mine. That he really is freaked out by roller coasters, just like in my screenplay version of this day.

"Close your eyes," I yell. "It'll go faster."

In fact, it's the fastest version of this ride I've ever been on. I spend the whole time watching Amir, his head rigid and locked, his eyes squinted into dots, Pittsburgh whirring by behind him like a blender that's full of something brown and green and occasionally blinking with tiny lights. It hurts my neck to look at him this way, and I don't even care. Frankly, I appreciate it. To be feeling anything again means I might still have a pulse. I missed my annual physical recently, so it's a legitimate question.

We whiz around the final bend. We pull back into the station. The Racer bell rings again, and I glance across the platform and watch as Geoff and Carly's car zooms ahead of ours at the very last moment, pulling into the station first, as it never has before in all my years of coming to Kennywood. My luck changed, or rearranged.

Their car is a fit of celebratory shouts.

"*Suckers!*" Geoff's saying, pulling up his lap bar.

"Come on," I say, tapping Amir's shoulder. "We're here. You survived."

"Did we win?" he says. He stands up. He opens his eyes and looks either hopeful or dazed. I'm going to say hopeful.

"Definitely," I say.

Five hours in and Geoff and Carly are off "scouting for corn dogs." But they're not scouting for corn dogs, not really, because Carly is a devout vegetarian. They're leaving me and Amir to find lunch on our own. This makes me nervous.

"So what's good here?" Amir says. We've been standing, silent, in a kind of epic outdoor food court line.

"The pizza is probably the safest," I go, watching Amir's face for the subtlest clues.

"Hmm," he goes, "I had a *lot* of pizza for dinner last night."

"Oh, no way."

"Way."

The guy two spaces in front of us is ordering the amount of food you'd stock up on for Thanksgiving, so I'm picturing how Mom might react if I ever brought Amir home for a holiday when I feel my butt light up like a Christmas tree, and realize Amir's hand is pressed into my lower back.

He's moving me up in line, but I pretend he's actually just dying to touch me.

The Thanksgiving guy departs with a teeming tray, and this little boy in front of us gets into an argument with his big sister about funnel cakes. Amir picks up on the thread with: "So, do *you* have any siblings?" and the question is so terrible and unexpected that I stare fuzzy eyed at the chalkboard menu as if it might turn into an old screenplay I can simply recite from.

"Uh, what?" I say.

"Do you have any siblings?"

I dare myself to look at him, and despite how hard I try to appear neutral, I must not succeed, because he throws his hands up and laughs and goes, "Wow, touchy subject! There's no right answer! I'm an only child myself."

Oh my God, he doesn't know. Carly didn't tell him.

I had imagined I'd be pissed at Carly for revealing all sorts of stuff about me to Amir, but I guess not. I guess she didn't tell him about December twentieth, the only interesting thing about me, anymore.

"Oh," I say.

"People always pity me for being an only child," Amir says, scratching his neck. I catch a glimpse of his armpit hair and it is black and without flaw. "But I love it."

He steps forward as the little kids in front of us teeter away with their own funnel cakes, their faces streaked with the tracks of drying tears. "How about you?" he goes.

But we're at the counter. *"Can I take your order?"* Thank God we are at the counter.

Somehow I murmur: "Burger and a large Coke, no ice," and Amir orders a cheeseburger without the bun, on "extra lettuce," and then he says to me, again, like he's the third Hardy Boy out to solve the mystery of my broken spirit: "You're avoiding this question. . . ."

I'm not sure if he pays or if I pay, only that we find a seat in the shade. I can't look at him, so I take such a big bite of burger that it makes Amir laugh. I would fill my mouth with moths and bees right now if it meant not having to speak.

When I finally swallow, after watching Amir negotiate his plastic fork around the lettuce, as if, with enough prodding, it might morph into something actually edible, like onion rings, I say to him, "I'm an only child, too," just like that.

And saying it makes it real.

"Hey," he says, holding up his bottle of water, "to not having annoying siblings!" I toast him with my Coke and swallow away the acid in my throat.

I just—I need to see if he actually likes me. I refuse to be his pity project. And so I am an only child now too, which is a version of the truth.

Geoff and Carly find us. Geoff is holding three corn dogs, and they look kind of amazing, and somehow Carly has tracked down a salad—which, at Kennywood, is approaching a "story of Easter" level of miraculous—and I'm instantly fine. With Geoff here I know my place. I'll be the guy who just makes comments from the sidelines, Donald O'Connor in *Singin' in the Rain*, even though I can't really dance. Let Geoff be Gene Kelly. (Famous Pittsburgher, by the way.)

We make fun of Amir for not ordering a bun, and he finally gives in to the rest of humanity and takes a chomp out of Geoff's third corn dog, and Carly calls us all brutes and spouts off some crap about how "the only reason meat tastes good" is because at the last minute, "animals are frightened" and release "a certain kind of enzyme" that adds to the flavor, and during this entire impassioned speech, Geoff begins a low *moo* that grows loud enough to attract the attention of the funnel-cake siblings, and what I'm getting at is that we're restored. That I'm okay again. That Amir is knocking his shin into my shin from across the rusty table, and that it's nice.

"Man, that's sad," he whispers. We've been carrying on about how Geoff's manager, Venessa, made him shave off his mustache, and so the laughing spills over when we turn around to see what Amir's looking at.

It's a lady and her family. The lady kind of looks like my mom.

"I honestly can't believe the way some people let themselves *go*," Amir says. "It sorta gives me the willies."

I stand up right away and say, "I have to go to the bathroom," and I'm probably just as surprised as anyone when I do.

But you know by now what I never do in front of other people.

And so when I've got my feet hiked up on the seat of this

dirty bathroom stall, I let the tears come—harder than the funnel-cake siblings', harder than the scared girl who ran out of the Racer line earlier, harder than how Geoff and my mom cried in our kitchen yesterday. Or was it the day before?

I guess I just didn't expect to find out that Amir is not, in fact, 100 percent ideal, this early on. Ha. How incredibly me. Too controlling. Too sensitive. Always just a little *too*.

I go to the mirrors. "Stop," I say at my reflection, which is tattooed and scratched with graffiti. "Stop," I say again, and this time I listen to the talking face that used to look like Quinn Roberts—the guy voted "cutest weirdo" in an unofficial poll conducted by the girls in middle school—and I stop crying, for him. For the cutest weirdo, and maybe the least likely to succeed now, too.

One little detour before rejoining my trio in the picnic area: "I really like your earrings," I say to the lady at the table, because she's got cool earrings on. I really do like them.

She sneers at me the way you do when your whole life is about being noticed for the wrong thing, and she doesn't say thank you, I think because she thinks I'm making fun of her, which I'm not.

I stand here long enough that the lady's husband, skinny just like my dad was, goes, "You have a *problem*?" But the lady puts up her hand to him and goes, "It's okay," because she must realize it *is*. That teenage boys who make fun of big ladies never stand around afterward, like I'm doing right now. Believe me, they ring your doorbell and they call your mom terrible names and then they run and they run, and they never dare to look back. And I hate them, and I've memorized their faces.

"Thank you," she says, touching one of the earrings. "My daughter made them for me."

When I get back to our table in the shade, which is somehow not in the shade anymore, Amir looks flat-out mortified, his brown face glowing pinker than a poker. I guess he didn't really notice my mom standing on our front steps when he picked me up this morning. I guess some people don't see everything. I guess Geoff and Carly told him about her, and me, while I was in the bathroom. And I wonder what else.

"Come on," I say. "Let's hit some more rides."

CHAPTER THIRTEEN

Our clothes are still damp from the log flume as we pull onto my street just before midnight. My fake glasses are fogged up and kind of smudgy, too. How do people manage to keep glasses clean all day?

"Okay, before you get out of my car," Amir says, turning down NPR, "you have to pass one round of Trivia." I like that he listens to NPR.

"Oh, boy," Carly goes, "the rare Trivia counterattack."

All I want is to be dead asleep.

"All right," I say, when it seems like Amir isn't kidding. I'm on the side of the car that doesn't open, anyway. So I'm kind of trapped, I mean.

"Name the horror franchise that was shot in Pittsburgh in the sixties," Amir says, "and was originally titled *Monster Movie*."

He's looking at me in the rearview mirror and I'm not looking away, which is something.

"Whoa!" Geoff goes, thumping his hands against the dashboard. "This dude *brought it*, Quinn."

"No," I say. "It's too easy, Amir. It's literally insulting. *Carly* probably knows the answer."

"Uh, I don't," she goes.

"Scoot," I say to her, and she opens her door and I hop out to the curb, which is still radiating such warmth that I actually look up, to make sure I'm not standing beneath a heat lamp of some sort. I'm not. We don't even have streetlights, ha.

Amir gets out and walks me to my mailbox, two feet away, which is kind of sweet.

"Quinn doesn't know the an-swer," he goes in this sing-song way.

"Quinn *does*, actually," I say, not in a sing-song way. "But that is some third-grade-level movie trivia you're rocking, and it's beneath me." I am terrible at flirting. I open the mailbox and then I shut it. "So, I should probably get inside."

"You're pretty smart."

I roll my eyes.

"You are," he goes. "I can't believe somebody so *not* ugly is allowed to be so smart. Frankly, I can't believe you're in *high* school."

"Neither can I," I say. "I can't believe high school is even legal, as a concept."

Yes, good line. Good line, Quinn. He's laughing.

"How do *you* know about movies shot in Pittsburgh, anyway?" I say. It's just unusual that anyone else who's even remotely cute and under the age of sixty would know this stuff.

"I took a horror film elective at Pitt this year," Amir goes, rolling his eyes just like I did. Nice to know that even college students are filling time with a good eye roll.

"Why the eye roll?" I go. "I'd kill to take a film course instead of, like, calculus. That sounds so fun."

"Yeah, well, that's it for electives for a while. My parents want me to buckle down next year. That's their term. 'Buckle down.' And 'pick a major.'"

Amir's face lights up bright and slick. It's my porch light, flashing on-off-on-off-on. I feel my ribs contract. I'm on the verge of being turned into a pumpkin.

"I have to get inside," I say.

"Okay," he says. "Oh—I wanted to send you that photo from Noah's Ark. You look *uh*-dorable in it."

Nice. I've advanced from "not ugly."

We took this selfie outside one of Kennywood's oldest attractions. Geoff insisted we all pose like animals. Geoff picked a flamingo (and he's the straight one), Carly picked a peacock, Amir was a wolf, and I picked a sloth.

"Sounds good," I say, wondering if Mom is watching us from the front window. Knowing she is, actually. In retaliation,

I dig my foot into the dirt, like I'm playing shortstop. Like I'm a regular local guy.

"What I meant," Amir says, "is do you have a *phone* number where I could *text* you the photo? I'll do it right now."

He reaches for his pocket, but: "*Oh*," I say, "I have to get a new phone. My old one is, like, busted." Pause. Like, you can hear actual crickets chirping out of tempo from the trees. "I dropped it in the toilet, I mean."

"Awkward," Amir says, and Mom flashes the lights again, and I say, "I'm gonna go. Thanks for the ride today."

"Hey, cutie," he goes, when I'm halfway up our crumbly cement stairs. I'm seeing them like I've never seen them before and I hate them. I bet stairs don't crumble in Dallas. I bet they're made of, like, granite. "Do you have any plans this weekend, other than for your birthday?"

I don't have plans for my birthday.

It would probably seem cool to say, *Yeah*, that *I've got lots of plans*—lots of plans, lots of dates, lots of demand. But "no" is all I can say, "I don't have any plans," because apparently saying I dropped my phone in the toilet used up all my lies for the night.

"Maybe we could, like, hang out tomorrow night or something?" Amir says. "I leave town next week."

My face does this extremely complicated thing from the old days known as smiling, and I go, "Okay." Okay.

Amir leaves my mailbox and opens the driver's side door

and says, "There's a foreign film festival in Shadyside. I'll find you online and send you the info and you can see what you think."

I catch Geoff looking up from his phone, and I can tell he wants to laugh so hard about two gay dudes who are *indeed* going to go see a foreign film, and even though I hate reading at movies, I think maybe this isn't an awful idea.

"Okay," I say again, but actually: Amir isn't going to find me online. I deactivated all my profiles three months ago. I was tired of getting tagged in #tributes. I was tired of the banal poetry and misappropriated quotes that people would add my name to and, worse, Annabeth's. *"This made me miss @annabeth_roberts17,"* some second-tier girl from school would say, tagging Annabeth in a ludicrous Eleanor Roosevelt quote written in, like, Comic Sans, and laid over a very fake-looking rainbow, as if @annabeth_roberts17 even liked rainbows. You know what Annabeth Roberts, seventeen, liked? Gray skies.

"So, next time I see you," Amir says, after I realize I've been standing here zoning out for, oh, ever, "you better know the answer to my Triv—"

"*Night of the Living Dead,*" I say. And then: "And it was originally called *Monster Flick,* not *Monster Movie.*"

He smiles. "You are so damn *smart.* Unfair. Blessed with hotness and smartness. You have the perfect life." And he gets into the car, and Carly turns to me and bops her eyebrows, and

Geoff flashes a peace sign at me (*that's* new), and I'm standing on our crumbly steps when I hear the front door click open and the low, throaty, phlegmy voice behind me appearing right on cue: "Who was that?"

"Nobody," I say to Mom, trying not to actually *float* by her. "Carly's new boyfriend."

Oh, never mind: I didn't use up all my lies tonight. Or maybe it's past midnight, and the lie meter has clicked over to tomorrow morning. More as this story develops.

"*Hmm*," Mom says, or at least I think she does. I'm too busy bounding up the stairs to switch on my laptop, to fire up ye olde wireless, to debate about reactivating my old accounts and rejoining the night of the living teenagers.

But the wireless isn't picking up. Our power may have gone out today—there was some weather in the area.

So I totally restart my computer, which I haven't actually done in ages. Since before, probably. And that means the first app that opens is my cloud storage, and *that* means the first thing I see when my computer screen flickers to life again is my Q & A folder, stacked with all our old movies, organized by genre, date, and length—each and every one shot in Pittsburgh. Our very own kind of monster flicks.

CHAPTER FOURTEEN

And sometimes you wake up at seven in the morning because somebody is *humming*. What the actual fuck.

I slide my laptop off my belly and head to where my new air conditioner *should* be, and when I look outside: Tiffany and Ricky's mom is in their yard, humming and weeding at seven in the morning, like this is some kind of David Lynch movie.

Let me describe the Devlins' house to you: exact same construction as ours, but theirs was the one that you went to on Halloween to get the full-size candy bars. Ours was the one you skipped, because Mom literally handed out dimes, from our animal-cracker barrel in the pantry.

God, it's early. And yet: I slip my mesh shorts on over my lucky boxers and I go outside and cross the street, and when Mrs. Devlin doesn't notice me, I clear my throat, like you'd do in a comedy.

"Oh, my gosh," she says, turning around and holding up one of those little hand-shovel things like she's Glenn Close in *Fatal Attraction*. "Quinn, you snuck up on me!"

"Sorry, Mrs. Devlin."

"Are you okay?" She stands up slowly. By now you'd think she would have lowered the weaponlike shovel. "You look so— Lord, you're a *man*."

"Um. It happens. If you're lucky!"

Weird laugh. "I love the glasses."

"Thank you," I say, touching the frames. They are really heavy. Like, I actually feel a little pain in my nose bridge, which is saying something because I've always felt that my nose is a little too big for my face. I'm delicate where I should be strong and I'm strong where I should be delicate. New theory.

"Should I let Tiffany know you're here?" Mrs. Devlin says, brushing clumps of dirt off an apron sort of thing. "She's asleep, but I'm sure she'd love to see you. It's been forever."

I should mention to you that Tiffany goes to boarding school now. She sort of cracked in eighth grade, the taunting about her sixth toe sending her over the edge the same year Ricky sold his first screenplay for like a million dollars (seriously). And so Tiffany got some kind of elective foot surgery to remove the toe, and then Ricky paid for her to go away to Michigan, to this school where you ride horses all day and they don't give you grades.

"Oh, don't worry about waking her up," I say. "It's super

early. I bet she was out late last night doing things those wacky kids like to do."

Mrs. Devlin does the adult version of laughing at a teenager's joke, which sounds like heat pipes being turned on for the first time after a long summer. All our summers are long. Same with our winters. "Tiff's boyfriend visited, from Michigan, so we all went to South Hills Village for dinner. It was fun. There's a new seafood place that's pretty goo—"

"Her *boy*friend?" I say, as if a high school girl with a boyfriend is such an earthshaking statistic.

"Yeah, they met at school."

It's just, Tiffany was always younger than Annabeth. And Annabeth never got to have a boyfriend. Doesn't seem right.

"He's a lovely young man."

"Is *he* inside?" I say, gesturing wildly as if they allowed a convict into the house. My brain can't keep up with the math that a six-toed girl has a lovely young man visiting her from Michigan and my sister is in an urn.

"No, no," Mrs. Devlin says. "We put him up for the night. He's at the Hilton on McMurray Road."

"That's cool," I say, like an idiot.

Mrs. Devlin walks down the little slope of their grass, meeting me on the sidewalk and putting her hair up in a ponytail. "Well, Quinn, I'm really glad to see you *outside*, finally." Some moms can still pull off the ponytail look.

"Yeah, I actually went to Kennywood yesterday, with Geoff

and some friends," I say, turning around and pointing at our house, as if *it* is a theme park. My geography is all off. That's when I notice these weird little black ribbons tied around the trees on our block. Huh. "It was fun."

"Was there something you wanted from *me*, hon?" Mrs. Devlin says.

"No, I just—last night I stayed up till like four, rewatching some of the movies we made in your yard, so, I don't know, I saw you out here and wanted to, like, look at it again. For old times."

She tilts her head at me. "Well, okay, hon. Feel free to hang out. I think I'll get back to my garden, though?"

"Yes!" I say, clapping once. "Of course. You do that. I'm gonna dash."

I turn and look both ways, as if you have to on this road (you don't), and just before I step off the sidewalk to head back up to my hot room and wonder why I came outside at all: "Oh, Quinn!" Mrs. D. says. "You'll be interested in knowing something."

I turn back around. "Uh-huh?"

"Rick's finally coming back to town!"

"Wait, Ricky *Devlin*?" I say, like a moron, but that's the only way I can picture his name. "Ricky Devlin" is always how you say his name, like he's Charlie Brown or something. Stop and picture it for a second: None of the other Peanuts ever calls him just Charlie. . . .

She giggles. "Yes, Ricky Devlin. My Ricky."

"Oh, wow. The golden boy returneth!"

"He and his partner are going to be here for two weeks while the movie shoots."

Brain. Overload. "I'm sorry, wait, what?"

Mrs. Devlin bounces the shovel handle on her hip. "Well, honey, didn't your mother tell you?"

I look back at the dangerous wooden roller coaster that is my house. "No," I say. "I mean, maybe she did. I've been forgetting things a lot."

Mrs. Devlin shakes her head. "Of course you have, hon. Of course you have." From this angle—with the sun coming up slow behind her chimney, and me knowing that Tiffany is asleep inside and that her boyfriend is staying down the road at a Hilton—Mrs. Devlin looks like a mirage.

"Ricky and his partner, Juan, are coming in from LA to be guests on the set of his movie. They're embroidering chairs for them and everything."

"The *No Such Thing As Fire* sequel?" I say. If this were a cartoon, my eyes would have bugged out of my head. But this isn't a cartoon, this is the live-action tragedy known as my life, and so my glasses have remained snugly in place.

"No, hon, this is something else. Very indie. Look it up online. The *Post-Gazette* did a huge piece; it was in *Variety*, the whole deal."

You *go*, Mrs. Devlin. I love that she's so Hollywood now,

she can't even bother to give me the logline to her son's newest movie—at seven fifteen a.m. on a weekday in the summer, by the way.

"Well, that's amazing." I scratch my arms. Apparently I'm covered in mosquito bites.

"They're looking for extras for a crowd scene this week, in Station Square," Mrs. Devlin says, finally turning around to head back to her precious weeds. "Maybe you and Tiffany could have fun in the background together, like the old days. I can ask Ricky."

"Almost like the old days," I say to Mrs. Devlin. "Except Annabeth won't be directing this one."

Unless she . . . will be? Somehow?

I actually stand here one second longer, because this news—that Ricky is actually gay, and that he's about to shoot an independent movie back home, when all his other films have been big-budget CGI cheese-fests—it's all such a crazy casserole of headlines that for all I know, Annabeth *is* directing it.

Annabeth's directing and Mom's playing the romantic lead.

And Dad's coming home, and not just to pick up his shorts.

And I'm happy again.

"No, that's right, hon," Mrs. Devlin says, yanking so many weeds at once that she accidentally pulls out the one, lone, robust flower, too. "Annabeth's not directing this one." She points over my shoulder, and I look back. "I think your porch lights are flashing."

CHAPTER FIFTEEN

You would not say Venessa is "thrilled" to see me, but I'm a paying customer and she can't kick me out. I think that's in the Constitution somewhere.

I take my iced coffee to the practically Parisian leather armchairs and wait for Geoff to bop over. Except he doesn't bop over. He walks over. "I seriously can't talk for long today," he says. "Venessa kinda rode me hard the last time you were here."

I *slowly* raise my eyebrows. "And you liked it."

"Quinn, come on."

Something's up when your straight friend doesn't laugh at sex references.

"Okay, I have a favor to ask y—"

"I can install it tonight," he says. "Like, I can bring it over after Family Dinner Night." This is a weekly thing in Geoff's house, even in summer. Can you imagine such traditions being performed without irony?

"Oh, the AC," I say. "Yes, I need that."

"Well, what *else*?" he says. He's being really impatient with me. Unusual. I kind of rely on Geoff for, like, all-you-can-eat niceness.

"Um, I was sort of hoping you could get a message to Amir, through Carly."

Geoff slaps his hands down on his green-aproned thighs. "Dude, seriously. This is like medieval times. This is embarrassing. You should just send a smoke signal or something."

"I'll buy a phone tomorrow. For my birthday. Happy birthday, me."

"No, you won't."

"I will, I will," I say. But Geoff's right. I won't. Also, my phone isn't even broken. I technically don't even need a new one.

Uh-oh. She's baaaack. *"Geoff."* Venessa heads to the fixings bar to refill the soy milk, and Geoff looks at her and then back at me, and goes: "Fine, I'll get one message to Amir, *one* more time. But that's it. What is it?"

"Why are you so pissed with me? Why are you being such a little *bee*otch?"

Geoff doesn't say anything. He just stands there with his lips pursed.

"Just tell him to, like, pick me up for the film festival

around seven tonight, outside my neighborhood—like, just before you turn in, after the Jiffy Lube on Willow."

"I *know* where you *mean*, Quinn."

"Jesus, okay."

Venessa clanks the soy milk down and turns to head back to the counter, and so I turn to head back to my bike. And right before taking off, I try to flash the all-new peace sign back at Geoff through the window, but he's not looking at me. He's pretending to wipe down the counter. But the counter was already spotless. I saw it. I see everything. It's the worst.

On my way home, I pull over and look for fireflies, but all I see is grass and litter, grass and litter, and I'm thinking maybe I never saw a firefly the other day to begin with. That maybe I'm the unreliable narrator of my own life.

I'm in our basement, which is twice as humid as New Orleans looks in *A Streetcar Named Desire*.

"It should be on top of one of the filing cabinets," Mom's saying from the top of the stairs.

She swears there's some old stationery down here, and she's anxious to write a note to Mrs. Devlin to thank her for organizing the black ribbons on our block.

"I'll find it, Ma. Just go back and watch your stories."

So she does. She takes off, and plumes of dirt rain down on me.

Apparently the ribbons went up on all the trees in January,

as an "awareness tribute to Annabeth" and to "driving safely," but neither Mom nor I got the memo.

Actually, we probably did—the mail upstairs is approaching a Pisa-level of tipping over on the counter, and I bet a community announcement went out and got lost in the pile—but we've still kind of refused to do anything but let it build up.

I'm making my way through brittle yellow stacks of newspaper clippings down here, old articles proclaiming my grandpa's latest patent. He's what you'd have called an inventor or an entrepreneur, which is French for: *never made enough money to leave Pittsburgh.*

Finally I see Mom's old stationery—her monogram printed in bumpy purple ink—and when I swipe it from the top of the filing cabinet, it leaves behind this dust-free rectangle on the glass of a framed photograph. It's of a beautiful woman on her wedding day. She is marrying a terrible man, who is annoyingly good-looking. Like: movie-star handsome; it's unfair. They are standing underneath a tree that looks like the tree we have out front, the one that Annabeth and I tied the stray dog to that we weren't allowed to keep.

But it isn't that tree. My parents got married in Ohio, after a lusty courtship. They went bowling on their first date, and my mom was so goo-goo over Dad, she wore the bowling shoes home and was fined twenty dollars. Why do people have to fall out of that kind of love? He is smiling so hard in this wedding photo.

"Something in the water in this town," Mom used to say, all those years later, when they moved to Pittsburgh and Dad wasn't smiling anymore, when he would come home from the office and disappear into the basement and not even care enough to slam the door. He wasn't even passionate enough to slam it.

What was he doing down here? We don't have a TV, or a carpet, or even finished walls. Was it just because this was the only place he could hide?

I'm thinking yes. I'm thinking yes, because that's kind of what I'm doing right now.

"Found it, Ma," I say, turning their wedding photo face-down on the filing cabinet, bringing the stationery up to her in the sunroom, and directing myself to *smile for her, dammit,* while I do it.

CHAPTER SIXTEEN

I spritz myself once with Dad's cologne. I swab my face twice with Mom's rubbing alcohol. I put on my only white collared shirt and then I spend fifteen minutes figuring out how to roll up my sleeves the "sexiest" way. No, I seriously Googled "the sexiest way to roll up sleeves," and got 2.3 million hits. *GQ* did a whole slide-show thing.

How is time so elastic that you can piss away an entire day and *then* be late for your first one-on-one date ever?

I'm leaping down the stairs three at a time when I note that Mom's barricading herself at the foot of them. There is almost a whole crash scene here, but she doesn't flinch.

"Will you put this in the mailbox for the morning?" she says.

"You mean just walk it across the street?" I say, taking Mom's card for Mrs. Devlin. You should see my mom's hand-writing. The thing is art.

"No, no, no," she says. "It's actually against the law to not mail a piece of mail. It's a federal offense to open a neighbor's mailbox."

Well, *that's* a new level of nuts. But I kiss her cheek and say, "No problem, Ma. I'll just put it in our mailbox. But *first*"—I pull a few newspaper clippings from behind my back, presenting them to her like an inky bouquet—"I thought you'd have fun looking at these. There's like a hundred piles of them in the basement."

She grins.

"It's a bunch of articles on Grandpa's inventions and stuff."

"Well, his almost-inventions. Nothing ever got off the ground." But you know what? She's not saying it like she's disappointed; she's saying it like she can't believe she doesn't reread these every day. This lifeline to a past when her life was still going to turn out nice. Maybe even mythical. The daughter of a mad, wealthy inventor.

"I've gotta jet," I say, "but don't read them all at once, or you'll get a toothache!"

No idea what that means, but I say it in that detective voice that always makes her laugh—and so I'm caught short when I rush by Mom to head out the door, and instead of giving me that signature chuckle, she just goes: "You're sure putting on a lot of cologne for *Geoff*, lately."

I don't even respond. I just let the door slam shut behind me. Then I stand on our crumbly porch and think, *Shit*, and I drop the card in our mailbox, and I keep walking.

. . .

Nobody wears watches anymore. I don't know what time it is, but I feel like I've been standing out here for longer than I should. I was already running late, I mean.

But you should see the sky tonight.

Screw your astrology apps. Screw your games. Look up sometime. There is a whole wing of positive psychology—my therapist told me—that says the greatest way to affect your outlook on life is to consider what you already have more than what you *don't* have. And so I might not have a cell phone on me, or a sister at home, or a Dad at all, or a future, but holy shit I have the sky.

A car pulls around the bend from Willow to Morrow, and even though it's too big to be Amir's old Saturn, I still find myself adopting an exaggeratedly casual posture, literally yawning as if I hadn't prepped for this date by putting on my best underwear (you never know?) and a white shirt and one exact spritz of Polo.

But it's not Amir.

The car kicks up enough dust to back me up into a neighbor's chain-link fence, and that sends their dog, Lucy, running up and barking at me.

"Quiet, Lu," I say, bending down. Lucy actually starred in a Q & A short. It was called *White Puff of Magic* (ugh, the titles), and even though it was only like six minutes, it was a pretty sweet and effective movie.

My latest film was the most ambitious. It was going to be a full-length feature. Annabeth shot the first four scenes last fall, and I looked at the footage and thought the whole thing felt too dark—it was meant to be a slightly black comedy, but it was coming off as super self-serious. So I asked Annabeth to reshoot, and she grunted in my general direction and said, "I'm in the middle of filling out my college applications, you ungrateful ingrate. How about you write that character recommendation I keep asking you for, huh?"

Annabeth had to include a couple of character recommendations from "adults in mentor positions" for her college applications. She asked her AP Psych teacher to write one for her, but Mrs. Wadsworth went: "I have to write about thirty of these every year, Annabeth, so what I'd ask is that you write a first draft, and I'll go from there. Okay?"

"But how am I supposed to know what's special about my own freaking character?" Annabeth said to me over and over this past fall—like a toddler, or a parrot—and I got the hint and promised I'd write one of the character recommendations for her, that Mrs. Wadsworth could just sign, if she wanted. That it wouldn't be a big deal. And then I just never did.

Brother of the year.

Lucy's little eyes go from yellow to red, possessed. The fence is suddenly lit up, and I realize the light is coming from behind me.

Still squatting, I turn to wave as Lucy trots away, and now I wonder: What the hell does it look like I'm doing?

"What are you doing?" Amir says, rolling down his window. He's not being mean, though. He's really just asking.

"Neighbor's dog," I say. Why did I let Lucy lick my hand? Am I now the kid who smells of mutt tongue and Polo?

I get into the front seat and it's set too far back, so that my already short-ish legs have miles to swim, and Amir goes, "Feel free to adjust the seat," and I go, "Okay, cool, 'cause I was, like," and then I don't have anywhere to go with that.

"Hi," he says, when I've pulled myself forward.

"Hi," I say.

"Sorry I'm late. You ready?"

"So ready."

And off to a Japanese film festival in Shadyside we go. I'm actually really excited—tonight they're screening *Seven Samurai*, a 1954 movie that kind of set the standard for modern action cinema. Amir already has the movie theater address plugged into this GPS thing on his dashboard and everything, which is really sweet. He's really planned this out and isn't, like, "acting cool." There's maybe nothing nicer than somebody just coming straight out and showing you they like you.

"Okay, can I start with an apology?" he says. "After you buckle up?"

He shifts gears and I'm thinking nothing is hotter than a guy who drives stick shift. "Sure."

"I'm really super embarrassed about what I said about overweight people."

"You mean how it gives you the willies?" I actually say. "It's okay. You didn't know."

"It's not okay."

We zoom by the Andersens' place, down the hill.

"I was just making conversation at lunch," Amir says. "I have this thing where when I'm nervous, I talk too much."

"I'm over it, seriously."

Amir turns onto Saint Clair. I'm sitting here in auto-copilot mode, coasting along on a path I've taken a thousand times, not thinking. But when we get to the fork where I found the firefly, Amir makes a right. He's heading toward the school.

"Oh, shit," I say, and he goes, "What? What?" and I go, "Uh, nothing."

Amir gets a text—I hear it buzz in his pocket—and he reaches for it and I can't help myself, I just can't, and I say: "Please don't look at that," and it makes him laugh, because even I can hear the pitch in my voice: the matronly timber, scolding a kid for doing what kids do.

"Okayyyy," he says, pushing buttons through his shorts to silence the phone. I hate that I've made this awkward. No—I hate that Annabeth has. "So . . . have you ever seen a Japanese film?" Amir goes. "I think I only saw the original *Godzilla* at a sleepover once, but it may have been one of the one *billion* remakes. . . ."

And there goes the library, and there goes the volunteer firehouse, and there goes the old putt-putt, and I can't look away, I can't look away. We pull up to the very red light that Annabeth ran, right outside the school, and as I'm staring and staring at the horribly specific and distorted portrait of Annabeth, Amir goes, "Yo, I'm sorry."

This almost snaps me out of it, but it doesn't, not totally.

"Sorry?" I say.

"For driving you *right* in front of your high school on sum-mer break." I check his face. Nope. No pity. "You must want to get as far away from it as possible!" He still doesn't know. They didn't tell him. Carly and Geoff have allowed that to be my final trick of the night.

"It's green," I say, when the light changes and reflects off his glasses. You can tell he really needs them, because, in the angle he's using to stare at me, his eyes take on this distorted old-fashioned-Coke-bottle quality. He really does need his glasses and I really don't need mine.

"The *light*," I say when he's still looking at me as if *I* am the dead kid whose face is spray-painted into the spackled wall of my school, "is *green*."

Somebody honks. Amir's engine revs up. We pull away, but my thoughts don't. My thoughts linger back at the school, like smoke. They smolder. And yet they are without heat. They are a fire without ashes. My thoughts are one great big nothing.

It takes us weirdly forever to find parking, and then the line to the front of the theater is Jack-Rabbit-roller-coaster deep, and so by the time we get to the ticket counter and find out they're down to one remaining seat, Amir looks like he's going to lose his mind.

"It's cool," I say, because it really is. I don't think I can handle a Japanese film right now. Anytime I have to read, my mind instantly wanders, and I don't want my mind instantly wandering. I want my mind instantly obliterated.

She just . . . she genuinely looked like a dog. My beautiful sister. As if an art director said to a gang of middle schoolers: *Please paint a dog on the side of the school and tie a black ribbon around its ears.* And voilà, they nailed it.

"Well, should we get a frozen yogurt or something?" Amir says, and yes, we absolutely should. That's a great idea.

I take the liberty of tasting three different samples at the yogurt place, and it isn't until I'm filling up my official froyo cup with way too many opposing flavors that I see what I'm doing: giving my brain an intentional overload. *"Yes,"* I just keep saying at the counter, when the girl asks which toppings I want, and so after graham cracker crumbs *and* this raspberry sauce thing *and* gummy bears *and* kiwi *and* white chocolate chips, Amir puts his hand very gently on my lower back, not like we're moving up in line but like he's saying, *That's enough, Quinn.*

And this is the moment I fall in love with him.

He pays for us. We find weird chairs that have these impractical little tufts of butt padding. Approximately one bite into my yogurt, I look at the thing as if I'm coming out of a particularly vivid hypnotism session, and I start giggling. It looks disgusting. "Holy shit."

"Is right," he says.

"What did *you* get?"

"An extremely sensible peanut butter and chocolate combo. Solid. Classic."

I instinctively reach my spoon across to try his. There isn't a person in my life who I can't do this with. My life is best friends or nobody. My life is Geoff.

Amir pulls his cup away. "Say please," he says in this twangy way that gives *please* like four separate syllables and gives *me* like one solid boner, and so I say, "P-l-eas-e," and take a bite. I don't even offer him any of mine, because, really.

"So where are you going next week?" I say.

"Wait, did Carly tell you I'm leaving town?"

"No, you did."

"Oh." He laughs too hard. Wasn't a good line and wasn't even a line.

The music in here is blasting, really blasting, so that I have to lean forward a bit to hear him. I'm okay with this.

"I got into this writing workshop thing," he says, rolling his eyes again. I want him to own how hot he is.

"Oh, no way."

"Way."

He eats frozen yogurt slower than anybody on earth.

"So, like," I say, "what kind of writing workshop?"

"Ah, it's lame. Do you read novels? Don't answer that. Nobody ever gives the answer I want."

Man, do I get that. Try being a screenwriter and watching your nearly perfect sequence get obliterated by a passing airplane, in the middle of a scene that's supposed to take place in the eighteen hundreds.

"I love novels," I say, loudly, louder than the music level even calls for.

"O . . . kay," he says, not believing me, which he shouldn't. I don't love novels, or: I don't like anything assigned to me.

Crap, now he's saying something about San Francisco.

"I love San Francisco," I say. Everything is love or hate with me these days. I hope I just like or dislike some stuff in my seventeens and eighteens.

Oh my God, I turn seventeen tomorrow. Holy shit, that sounds old.

"Oh, you've been to SF?" he goes, but I haven't been, and this brain-freezing business is no joke. I shake it off.

"Sorry. I'm, like, distracted by how cold this is." I hold up my goop. We laugh. "I've never been to San Francisco, but there's a *preeetty* campy Bond scene filmed there, over the Golden Gate Bridge, which you have to visit."

"Bond?"

"*James Bon*—oh. Ha-ha."

He set me up. Clever guy.

"Anyway," he goes, "my writing workshop isn't in San Francisco proper. It's going to be farther down on the peninsula."

I've never totally understood peninsulas. It's like: Are you an island? Pick what you are, peninsulas!

I've spaced out again. He's staring at me. "I'm sorry," I say, too confidently tossing my cup across the room and absolutely missing the garbage can by nothing less than a yard. We crack up. I pick it up, wipe off my hands, and turn back to see Amir making a big frowny face and pointing at my stomach. When I look down, there is a full-on gummy worm attached to my shirt by means of chocolate sauce.

"Oh, no way," I say at my shirt.

"Way," Amir goes. Somehow, in the span of twenty seconds, he's acquired a little thing of warm water and a towel from the front counter. He's squatting low, dabbing at my shirt and kind of fixing me up. It is the sweetest thing.

"I think that should take out most of the stain," he says, looking up at me.

Some bro-types are leering at us, and Amir says, "Shall we?" and motions to the door, and I say, "Duh," and we're on the muggy street in two seconds flat.

"You said you were sorry back there," Amir goes, "immediately after you spilled chocolate sauce on yourself like an adorable invalid and directly before we were nearly hate-crimed into the history books."

"Whoa, you *are* a writer," I'm saying, but really I'm stalling, because I can't remember what I'm sorry about. So much, really. Everything.

"Ha," he goes. "Don't tell my straight-ass parents I'm a writer. They think I'm going to San Francisco to intern for a startup. They don't approve of my clandestine plan to write the great Iranian-American novel, heh."

It's coming to me now. When I was zoning and brain freezing, he mentioned San Francisco in regards to this writing program. I can fake this.

"So . . . will you know other people . . . at the, like, your writing program?"

"Eh, I can tell you more about the program later. We should decide what we want to do tonight."

Oh, that's nice. I thought that yogurt and a wardrobe malfunction was sort of "it" for our first date.

"Crazy idea," Amir says, grabbing my shoulder and steering me into an alley between two brick buildings. Oh my God, is he going to kiss me? Is this it? I still have gummy bear, etc., breath. "Do you like to bowl?"

I hate to bowl. But the poetry of it all. Mom beating Dad on their first date.

"I. Love. Bowling," I say, and Amir takes my hand, and a field of fireflies appears inside my chest and they all light up at once.

CHAPTER SEVENTEEN

We're three rounds into bowling and I don't really totally understand how the scoring works, but for whatever reason I've been able to turn this into a running bit, like I'm Goldie Hawn in some eighties screwball comedy.

"You're up," I say to Amir, after another of my bowling balls goes straight into the gutter. I did not inherit my parents' genes for this pastime, and in one brief, shining moment, I wonder if perhaps I am adopted. Somehow that would make Annabeth's death feel not so personal.

Amir has a whole stance and everything, where he holds the ball close to him like the thing is a fragile baby, and when he releases it, he grunts a little—*not* as a joke—and the ball knocks down five of the pins, which for me would be cause to go to Disney World, but seems to genuinely bum him out a bit.

"I thought that was a triumph," I say, but his "Thanks"

suggests he's a straight-A student who's never happy with anything but the best. Jesus. Wait'll he sees the *inside* of my house.

"Were you a straight-A student in high school?"

"Still am," he goes, sitting down again. His shirt is a little too tight and his chest strains against it, and I'm saying this is a great thing.

"That's gotta be a lot of pressure."

The group next to us lets out the kind of whoop and hoot that only Pittsburghers know how to do. Seriously, you wouldn't believe the pride and commitment to sports if you didn't live here, and even then.

"Quinn," Amir says, poking my knee with his finger.

"Yeah?"

"I said, You've gotta be a pretty good student, too, right? I mean, you're so quick."

"You should see me in gym class. I could challenge that notion."

"Ha, see. Quick."

I don't need Amir knowing how I just coast by academically, so I do that thing where I pretend to cough.

"Do you want some nachos or something?" Amir goes, and I say, "Or something," because I like when dialogue echoes in movies, but I'm secretly hoping he really does bring back nachos specifically.

He walks away and I study him. I'm the only person in this incredibly loud bowling alley who doesn't have his phone out, multitasking. Amir's jeans are just a little too baggy, so when they hang down, some underwear is sticking out, and it's the boxer variety, which just drives me delirious.

"Nachos," he says, back with a plate of the grossest and most wonderful looking dinner I've had in a while. "Do you like jalapeños?"

"Love 'em," I say, because I like them.

"Okay, go to town," he says. "Jalapeños, licorice, humidity."

"Things you hate?"

"Bingo."

A group of not-naturally-blond girls stumble into our area, and I feel offended, somehow, but when Amir leaps up and goes, "Would you guys like this lane? We're just having a snack," somehow I end up liking them.

"Cool, whatever," one of them goes, followed by a chorus of "Whatevs, sure," and Amir and I are taking the nachos to a little snack bar area that feels a million miles from the school cafeteria.

"So, what do they *want* you to do?" I say. Dammit, Quinn, set him up better. You're getting all "Geoff" with your lack of context.

"What does *who* wan—"

"Yeah, sorry, sorry, I should have set that up better. What do your parents want you to, like, study?"

He runs his hands through his mop-head. "Oh, them."

"I mean, we don't have to—"

Crunch. Crunch. Nachooooos.

"No, it's fine. It's fine. My dad's in finance and my mom is a fund-raiser on the Dallas scene."

"Oh, cool," I say.

"Yeah, cool if I go into finance."

"Have you always wanted to be a novelist?"

"Ever since I read Roald Dahl, yeah."

"*Willie Wonka and the Chocolate Factory!*"

"Actually, Charlie *and the Chocolate Factory*. I think *Willie Wonka* was just the film title."

"Oh," I go, "right."

Nothing, followed by nothing, and then: "What are your other favorite movies that were books first?" he says.

He has had three chips, total. I have had something like a thousand.

"Well," I say, "there are the obvious ones: *The Shining*, uh, *Carrie, Talented Mr. Ripley. . . .*"

"So are you just crazy obsessed with movies or do you actually want to make them someday?"

Wow. I'm a little insulted and don't even have a right to be. If I don't tell him about Annabeth, I can't be pissed he doesn't know about Q & A Productions, but this is my thing about why I think relationships—boyfriends, friends, anything—are such a hassle. I've lived for almost seventeen *years*. That is *so much* to catch somebody up about. I want people just to arrive in my life fully informed of my tastes and fears. The lists are pretty short, definitely memorizable. I wish they could be distributed to would-be suitors ahead of time, so they could rule themselves out. Or in! I'm open to "in," too!

"Uh, yeah," I say, "I guess I'd like to make movies someday."

I discreetly check my shirt and notice only the chocolate ghost stain, with no nacho cheese sauce in sight, and when I look up again, Amir goes, "Can I get you a drink?" But his eyes are shiny shiny shiny, like there's another set of eyes behind them. He's up to something.

"I'm good, thanks," I say, holding up a bottle of water.

"No, I mean," he goes, leaning in on his elbows. His T-shirt tugs at the collar. His chest. He has a really nice chest. You could land a helicopter on it. "Do you want a beer?"

I try to play it cool. I so want a beer. I also don't want to get in trouble or caught or something. I'm already out way too late, already worried my mom has called Geoff's mom, asking where he and I went to dinner.

"Definitely," I say, just like that, loud, and he slaps his hands down on the table and goes, "Cool."

I watch his baggy jeans and tight T-shirt walk away, and I'm looking at my forearms and thinking how hairless and sticky they are, on account of this disgusting table, and he's back faster than I could have guessed. Time is relative, these days.

"At your service, *monsieur*." Amir places the plastic cup

down in front of me, and perhaps he is a secret magician, because as I reach for it, he says, "Go slow," as if he absolutely and without a doubt knows this is my first beer ever.

I'm sipping and sipping and waiting for it to be good, and I go, "How about you? Favorite book-to-movie adaptations?"— and, by the way, Amir's slow about eating food, but half his beer is gone in two gulps.

"See, I don't have your extensive knowledge," he goes. "I think the only adaptation I'm confident I've seen is *The Ten Commandments*," which is a pretty good joke, so I throw it a laugh.

I take another sip of beer. Nope. Still gross. "Hey," I go, "will you look a movie thing up? On your phone?"

"Sure, *Mom*," he says. My face can't hide any lies, so Amir goes, "I'm teasing, Quinn," really soft and sweet, and he taps his knee into mine under this table and goes, "Okay, what am I looking up?"

"Okay, Google 'Ricky Devlin new movie.'"

"Who's that?"

"Oh, just some guy." A golden guy. "Like, an old baby-sitter."

The screen above our heads is broadcasting this vintage Pittsburgh Pirates game—it's like a twenty-four-seven loop of the "best games ever"—and there's a table of guys two nachos over who are reacting to it as if in this very moment they can't believe the home run that is currently being home runned.

"Okay, there's a bunch of results," Amir goes. "You want to see?"

I take a really big swig of beer, developing a new theory that maybe it tastes better in large quantities, and when that proves false but exhilarating, I burp a little as I'm saying, "No, just read one to me," and he goes, "Easy, slugger."

I put the beer down and pick at my nails. Difficult, as they're already nearly picked to kingdom come.

"Okay, so, here's something from *Deadline*, a few months ago—"

"Perfect, yeah, read that."

"'*No Such Thing As Fire* and *Battle-Ax III: Scorpion's Fury* screenwriter Ricky Devlin's spec script, *South Hills Apprentice*, was acquired by Relativity Studios in a deal brokered by WME. Script centers around a college dropout, home for the summer, who develops a bond with a complicated, antisocial child—and ends up learning lessons about death, life, and'— *hey*." Amir looks up from his iPhone. "You have a little something."

I can't tell what he means about the little something. I am only puzzling together that *I* am the complicated, antisocial child around whom this screenplay is based, and that perhaps this sounds like the worst movie ever. How could Ricky Devlin be dumb enough to write an autobiographical screenplay about us and actually *sell* the damn thing?

Amir's reaching across and swiping something from my lip,

and I wince away. I wince away. Just like Geoff did to my mom on the counter.

"It's just a beer mustache," Amir says, putting his phone on camera mode and flipping it to show me. I look like some "math nerd" in a porn—these ridiculous glasses, this haircut utterly lacking in style, this white froth mustache foaming me up like some kid Einstein.

Oh my God. *Kid Einstein.* One of my first movies ever with Annabeth.

I had this idea: What if Einstein and Freud and Hitler and Earhart (Amelia) had all been kids together, what if they'd been in school together? Kid Einstein, Kid Hitler, Kid Freud, and Kid Earhart, who'd be played by nobody, because the joke was: Even in middle school, Amelia Earhart was always missing.

"What if we don't cast anybody?" Annabeth offered, after I read her the first draft of my script. Always her, only her. "What if we cut all of Amelia's scenes?" It was her idea. All my best ideas were actually her ideas. Did you know that?

Oops. My beer's all gone.

"Hey," Amir says. He's next to me on this sticky banquet. Everything is sticky. His arm is around my shoulder, and I can smell his deodorant. I want to be attracted to this. I should be, but I'm not. He's my exact same height, but he's so much stronger than I am that I feel like he could crush me, and I know that seeing Annabeth's face on the side of the building should have wrecked me tonight but it didn't. It numbed me. What's wrecking me is the breathtakingly stupid stuff. The stuff I don't plan on—how Annabeth is the only person in the world who would appreciate a Kid Einstein reference. How she's the only person I'd be brave enough to share a first draft with.

"I want another beer," I say, and Amir, who's doing that super-gentle shoulder rub maneuver where just a guy's thumb is going up and down, goes, "Aw, Win, maybe that's enough for tonight?"

I whip my head so hard to look at him that our glasses almost smack, and I say, "What did you call me?"

"Um, *Win*. You know, short for Quinn, I guess?"

That's what she called me. That was ours; she called me Win and nobody else did, and I want to stand up and knock this table over and eat everybody's nachos and run out of this place screaming, but instead I play it like a Western and I grit my jaw and I say through my teeth: "I would really like another beer." Amir scoots over to say, "Here, you can finish mine and then we should go," and I don't even wait for half the sentence to be gone before I'm gulping his down, and you know what? My theory is right. At a certain moment, when you drink through enough of it, beer starts to become a kind of buzzing neutral.

"Whoa, there," Amir says when I leap up and knock my hip really, really hard against the edge of the table. I think the sound escaping me is a laugh, but oh God, it's not; it's the weak inbred cousin of laughter, and I don't do this. I only cry alone.

The table next to us has left behind a bunch of half-empty

beers, and, ladies and gentlemen, guess who chugs them all, one after the other, germs and dignity be damned?

Twenty seconds later Amir's got me under his arm, limping a little bit to the parking lot. I should probably be thankful that he is sweet enough to smile at me and say, "That's amazing, you've still got the little beer mustache going," but instead of thinking it's sweet, I'm just seeing *Kid Einstein* on the megaplex screen of my mind, and I say, "I think I need to go home." And other than Amir buckling me in, that's the last thing I remember.

CHAPTER EIGHTEEN

According to local sources, I slept in my bathtub last night.

"Jesus," I say, "*Christ.*"

This is the kind of hangover people write horror movies about, movies that are never funded because they're too graphic. If you don't know what a hangover feels like, congrats. You are smarter than I am. It's like a sledgehammer eloped with a swing set and they honeymooned in your head.

I lift my foot to turn the water on with my toe, and after it cools down a bit, I let it drench my legs. That's when I notice I'm still in my one good pair of underwear, and just that.

"Um . . . Amir?" I call out, louder than a smart kid would. These walls are so thin. Mom can probably hear every last detail of my life.

Nothing. Okay, so he's not here. Oh my God, thank God.

When my legs have been chilled enough so that I guess

they start circulating the blood back up in a way that's vaguely "refreshing," I see the pile of last night's cologned clothes, sitting next to the commode. Something is sticking out of the pocket of my jean shorts, which are hanging off the toilet plunger.

The glamour of it all.

I reach for my shirt so I can dry off my hands, and when I pull the note out of my shorts, I discover a message written in small, serial-killer block letters on thick graph paper. The paper of somebody who wants to be remembered.

"Win, if I can call you that?" Hoo boy. I turn the water off to prep for this moment. *"Thank you for being so honest with me last night. Thank you for feeling comfortable enough to cry in front of me. Feel better. Sleep it off. Let's hang again before I go west, young man. —Amir."*

And then: *"P.S. Thank you especially for finally telling me about your sister."*

Oh God.

I place the note on the lid of my toilet. I hold my breath to dunk my head under, and I am forced to wonder how long it might take to drown. Not that I'd have the nerve for it. Please, I squeal when I pop zits.

So when I'm up again, and cradling my face in my hands, the weight and the throbbing of all these questions begin to push through and pool at my eyelids, and the first question I'm seeing is: What *did* I tell him last night, about Annabeth, on the ride back to my house? Does he now know the things only the police and my mom and my therapist know?

I try to stand but it doesn't work out so hot, and so I'm back to sitting with all these thoughts about so many different maybes, which crowd into one another like horrible party guests making trouble in a bathroom.

Maybe I finally told somebody about how I had gotten into a huge fight with my sister on the morning of December twentieth, about how she was prioritizing everything else—including, of course, her college applications—over shooting my unfinished screenplay last fall.

Maybe I told Amir how I sent her a text that day, after she stopped me in the hallway outside calculus and said: "I'm canceling the shoot after school. I'm free last period and I wanna do some Christmas shopping," and my temper revved up zero to red-hot, and I said: "I can't believe you. I bet the *Coen* Brothers would never cancel an important shoot day," and Annabeth snorted and said: "We're not the Coen Brothers. They co-direct their films—*and* they finish their screenplays first," and my teacher said: "Class started thirty seconds ago, Mr. Roberts."

And maybe I told Amir that the text I sent to Annabeth after our fight that day was something like "**YOU'RE DEAD TO ME,**" and by "something like" I mean *exactly* like.

We texted constantly, so when she didn't reply to "**YOU'RE DEAD TO ME,**" I wrote back "**ok ok ok i was kidding jeez.**" When she finally did text me back that afternoon, I turned off my phone in a huff, without even reading it. Without realizing it would be her last text ever.

I get up from the tub, slow with plenty of shakes. My underwear is so heavy with water that I feel as if I'm in diapers. I wish I were. The chance to start over.

"Quinny," I hear Mom say quietly from the bottom of the stairs. "Come on downstairs. Somebody's got a surprise at the front door."

I towel down. I hate surprises. I throw my wet underwear in the sink and I head to my closet, not to get changed but to grab that film competition application from the top of my untouched textbook pile.

"One sec, Ma."

I put on my maroon robe and walk the application to the toilet, to brush Amir's note to the floor and to flip open the lid and to flush my half-finished summer plans down the drain, where they belong. And as I'm watching it try to fight and struggle to swirl away, I'm wondering one more *maybe* about last night.

Did I tell Amir the big act break, the big drama of my life story? That Annabeth was killed right after sending one last text to somebody in her phone listed as "Win"?

"Do you folks know who a 'Win' might be?" the police asked Mom, that night, when they showed up after school to find half the neighborhood ladies huddled around her in the kitchen. A coalition of moms, each of them happier than the next not to be mine.

"Do you folks know who a 'Win' might be?" they asked, and my mom looked up and said, "That's what Annabeth called her brother."

I was already upstairs with my earplugs in, never having turned my phone back on after school—but Mom has told and retold her version of the story to me as if I'll come up with an alternative ending to it. The definitive director's cut. The one that leaves the audience smiling instead of stunned.

I wonder what Amir actually thinks of me now—the light-weight who turned himself into an only child. The boy whose big sister coasted out of the last period of the day and right through a red light while sending one last message to me. A message that not even my mom has seen; that I *still* haven't had the guts to turn my phone on and read, calcified and preserved somewhere in my room like the only pirate treasure you'd never want to find.

I tie the robe shut, hide Amir's serial-killer note under my pillow, and exit my bedroom—but not before nearly tripping over a pair of bowling shoes, which are sitting by my door like polite foreign exchange students on the terrible summer immersion trip that is my life. I must have accidentally worn them home last night. Like mother, like son.

"Qui—"

"I'm *coming*," I say to her, heading down to my first morning as a seventeen-year-old.

CHAPTER NINETEEN

So, Geoff is standing at the front door holding an ice cream cake. That is happening.

"I don't like ice cream cakes," I say to him, like a jagoff. You think hangovers are going to be a joke, and then . . .

"I know," he says, holding it out. "It isn't *from* me."

I squint at him, and then Mom's behind me like an annoying sidekick, with: "That's the Geoff I know, face clean as a baby's butt."

"I don't think babies' butts are really all that clean, Mrs. R.," Geoff says, rubbing the place his "mustache" used to occupy. Geoff has been kind of a dick to me these last couple days, but now he's looking at Mom like the two of them used to have an act on a cruise ship.

I look through the plastic packaging of the cake box: HAPPY BIRTHDAY, WIN is spelled out in frosting, and it takes my breath away. Seriously, it's like the cake steals my breath, like some children's book villain, and I think: *Did my sister send Geoff a message from the grave, to deliver to me?* Unlikely. The two of them were always at each other's throats.

"Well, let me put that in the freezer so it doesn't melt," Mom says, taking the cake from me and making her way into the kitchen and then back to the sunroom. My hands are cool and my head is hot. Also, Annabeth knows I hate ice cream cake, so:

"Amir asked me to buy it for you," Geoff whispers.

"Well, ask Geoffy to come in, birthday boy!" Mom shouts.

But he stays put. "It's cooler out here," he goes, leaning in and looking past my shoulder. "What is your mom *doing* in there?"

I hear it, too—some kind of rhythmic ripping of fabric. Every few months Mom goes through a crafts phase.

Ignore. "So, wait," I go, stepping outside and letting our screen door *thwap* shut behind me. "Amir, like, asked you to buy me an ice cream cake?"

"Yup," Geoff says, blocking the sun. His eyes are the bluest blue. Leave it to a straight boy to have the most classic features and then squander them with terrible gold neck chains and jeans choices. "He said: 'Go get one of those Carvel cakes, but have them do a million flavors that don't really go together. It'll make Win laugh.'"

And so I laugh. "Oh, yeah—long story involving crazy froyo choices. From last night."

"Wow, you already have inside jokes. Also: Wow, I thought only Annabeth called you Win."

Now I shield my eyes too. "She does. I mean, she did, but he kind of came up with it too."

"Also, *also*: Wow," Geoff says, bypassing my various contributions to this conversation, "you're standing outside in a bathrobe. And you stink. I can't believe you got wasted for the first time without me."

"The other day you didn't care about coming in on me naked in the shower. Now you're judging me in a bathrobe."

"That was different. This is in public."

A crow flies by us, and we smile at the idea of my street being somehow "exposed." All that's missing around here are tumbleweeds and those zombies. And a lemonade stand.

"I gotta jet," he says. "You know Venessa."

"Aw, I was hoping you could help me put in the AC." Nothing. "Man, that lady is *tough* on you."

"You have no idea."

Mom's back, talking through the screen behind me. "What are you two doing out here? There's birthday cake to be eaten."

"It's not even noon, Mrs. R.!"

"That's never stopped me before!"

She has a way of sounding proud about these sorts of

statements, as if you can't get to be her size without a strangely American version of discipline. Which, let's be honest.

"Thanks for the cake," I say to Geoff, and I try to twinkle a secret separate thanks to Amir. We'll see how that plays out.

"Oh," Geoff goes, "something else. *Not* from you-know-who. It's from *me*, just so you know who to give credit to."

He runs to his car and scurries back with something from the front seat. I hate that Mom's witnessing all this.

"What the heck," I say, eyeing a small package in a little pink bag. Suspicious. It's as un-Geoff as it comes.

"It's a regifted bag," he says, his voice cracking, not out of emotion but out of growing up, "but the gift is new."

"Look at that," Mom says, right over my shoulder. God, does this lady love anything pink.

"Mom, aren't you *busy* cutting me *breakfast* cake?" I say, and she does her version of dashing away to leave us alone. "Aw, man, G-force," I say, unwrapping the present. "You really didn't have to get me this."

"Yes, I did. This will be cheaper than the amount of gas I've purchased, delivering you messages and, like, cakes."

He heads back to the car.

"I thought you refilled the tank for free at your dad's dealership."

"Yeah, well, speaking of my parents," he says. "You can thank them. My mom insisted I buy you that cell phone. It's been freaking her out not to hear me laugh around the house."

"What do you mean?"

"Nobody sends me funny text messages anymore," Geoff says, and he starts his Corolla and drives away.

"So, one more time: You're ruining your favorite black dress because why?"

We've eaten half the cake already, and it's a big cake. We're also standing at our kitchen island, as if by not sitting, we're somehow actively counteracting the calorie load.

"I want to cover all the trees in our yard with these scraps." This means Mom wants me to. She hasn't been outside for longer than five minutes since December. "I want us to have a mini-forest of ribbons. It will be beautiful."

"Why don't I just ask Mrs. Devlin for some extra ribbons? I'm sure she has them. They organized the damn tribute."

Mom's eyelid quivers. Stupid, Quinn. This is the first project Mom's had in a while, and she wants to defend herself, but I can see the words getting stuck in her lips like leaves in a gutter that Dad isn't around to clean out anymore.

So I write the line for her.

"*Actually,*" I say, "I can see why you'd want to use your black dress fabric. That way it's more of a personal effort."

She breathes again. "That's right. That's right." And holds up the torn remains.

"Want some more cake?" I say, side-eyeing the stuff like we're in an abusive relationship. My stomach hurts. My everything does, but I'm also the best kind of distracted.

"No thanks," Mom says, wiping the corners of her mouth with a paper napkin and smiling big. "Do you want to hear about your birthday gift now or later?"

"Um, wow. Maybe . . . now? No, later! It'll give my day a sense of purpose."

Really, I'm sort of dying to activate this phone and text Amir.

"Well, okay," Mom says, pressing her thumb into cake crumbs that have settled into the counter grout. "But can I give you a preview?"

"Previews," I say, "are my favorite thing." And then I switch to my movie-trailer voice, which always gets her. "*In a world* where movie trailers are better than the movies they are actually previewing," I say, and she giggles and we're good.

"Well, I found *this* stuck between two sheets of Grandpa's old newspaper," Mom says. She pulls forth a deeply yellowed twenty-dollar bill. It looks really old-timey, almost like funny money from the Wild West. "It's yours," she says, laying it in my palm. "And I'm feeling real inspired. I'm going to go through *everything* in this house and start clearing stuff out and just, I don't know . . . Maybe there's more treasure to be found in this old shack yet."

"Or bills to be paid," I mutter, putting my hand on the stack. It is now above my head on the counter, a practically comical sight if you believe that pain is an essential element to laughs. Which, by the way, I do.

"Happy birthday, my handsome little man," Mom says, kissing me on the cheek.

I'm three steps out of the kitchen, wondering what my first text to Amir should be, when Mom calls out, "There's Advil on my shelf in the medicine cabinet, Quinn. Don't take that useless store-brand stuff on Daddy's."

I guess I really do stink and look awful, because when I put my foot on the first step, she also says, "Be careful?" Be careful.

I think she means just the general *Be careful* of knowing you're seeing your only son hungover for the first time and don't know how to talk about it, so you'll just give advice on how to treat it, once he's safely out of eyeshot. Or maybe she means *Be careful* about other stuff. Be careful about following too many of your instincts, about falling in love with someone who loves you less, about being too wisecracking or smart-alecky or forthcoming with your heart. Basically be careful about being you. You're only a Roberts, after all.

"I will, Ma," I say, "I'll be careful," just as I'm tearing open the cell phone box and slicing an epic cardboard paper cut into my hand. But: Ignore, because I am so thankful my new phone is an entirely different model than I or Annabeth ever had. (I used to have a Droid. Maybe all I need to be happy again is a new operating system.) I don't need any more reminders of the past. My life is all future now. All future, all the time. Watch out.

I trudge up the stairs and into my room, typing "There's

1/2 an ice cream cake with ur name on it," to Amir. And then I punch in his number from my corkboard and hit send before I can talk myself out of it.

My hand is really bleeding now, but then, almost right away, I get an immediate response—so immediate it's not even cool, it's just nice—and it says: "**Glad to see you've joined the land of the living this morning. Chase the cake with some Advil. Coming to my party tonight?**"

I don't have any idea what he's referring to, but also: My hand doesn't even hurt, at all. Amir must have mentioned a party to me last night. Probably right after I cried in front of somebody for the first time in forever.

"**Wouldn't miss it,**" I type, and I smile and hit send at the very same time.

CHAPTER TWENTY

I'm in our yard, tying one of Mom's black dress scraps to our birch tree, when this hot-looking car pulls onto our street and kicks up dirt and silently maneuvers onto the Devlins' driveway. Yeah, it's one of those silent cars. The little ones that look like they're made in Japan or maybe California.

I try to make myself as small as possible, crouching low.

Ricky Devlin—it's gotta be Ricky Devlin—gets out of the front seat, and then a small handsome man gets out too. It's gotta be Juan. I think that's what Mrs. Devlin called him. It's clear Juan has never been to the Devlins'—has any brown person ever been to our block, other than Amir?—because Ricky Devlin comes around and takes Juan's hand and starts walking him to the front door. Before they knock, midway up their brick path, Ricky Devlin puts his hands on Juan's waist and has "a talk" with him. I know the look.

EXT. DEVLINS' HOUSE - DAY

RICKY DEVLIN (30ish, still handsome, still
golden) and JUAN (mid-twenties, good-looking
bartender type) stand outside the house,
considering it.

> RICKY DEVLIN
>> I promise they're going to
>> love you.

> JUAN
>> Have they ever met a boyfriend
>> of yours before?

> RICKY DEVLIN
>> I've never technically *had* a
>> boyfriend before.

Juan rolls his eyes and nervous-laughs.

> JUAN
Oh, boy. This could be a disaster. If your mom
calls me your "friend," I'm outta here.

                    RICKY DEVLIN
          Hey, have I ever been wrong
          before?

                       JUAN
          Yes. You told me we'd be
          engaged by now -- after the
          last movie premiere.

There's a strange pause, and then a pickup
truck passes the house and Ricky Devlin backs
away from Juan -- practically pushing him into
the bushes.

                       JUAN
            Jesus, Ricky.

                    RICKY DEVLIN
          I'm sorry, sweets. I'm jumpy.
          This isn't West Hollywood.

When the truck passes, he kisses Juan, deeply
and almost too forcefully. They turn to head
to the front door, but Ricky Devlin's gaze

lingers on the street, watchful and nervous
of being back on this block.

Or maybe he's looking for Quinn, his South
Hills apprentice.

I wait for Ricky Devlin to kiss Juan. I wait to see a truck pass, to see what will happen. I wait for the tears to come, or the drama. But they don't. All that happens is: Tiffany opens the door—looking beautiful and, somehow, utterly first-tier—and she screams Ricky's name, and he bounds up the steps to hug her.

Their front steps aren't crumbling; they are totally intact. Juan follows. And then, wonderfully, Juan steps up to Ricky Devlin's side, and Ricky Devlin takes Juan's hand and gives it a peck, right in front of Tiffany.

I hear her give a "Whoo-hoo!" kind of siren call.

When they head inside, I do too, and as I pass through our foyer, Mom catches me by surprise, bird-watching the whole scene from behind the windows of what in a normal house you'd call a sitting room and in our house is where cardboard boxes go before being recycled.

"Well, Ricky sure grew up," she says, still staring outside.

"I tied a ribbon for Annabeth," I say, hearing my new phone ring upstairs and brushing past Mom and changing the subject all at once, like the world's greatest multitasker.

CHAPTER TWENTY-ONE

Win, *hey, it's Amir. I'm gonna keep calling you Win until you tell me not to. Um. Hey! Look at me, leaving a voice mail like it's the eighteen fifties. My mom would be proud of me. For once. Ha-ha. Okay, here are the deets on the party, because they just changed and I don't have your e-mail and it's too much to text. . . ."*

The Ephron sisters were famous for wry films made before I was born. One of the sisters wrote, the other one directed, and it really worked out nicely. Big box office. Introduced Tom Hanks and a lady named Meg Ryan to the public as that decade's go-to romantic pair. The Ephron sisters were cool. They were trendsetters.

The Coen Brothers don't need an introduction, unless you think they do, in which case I'm not even sure I want you reading this.

The Nolan brothers are a different, darker kind of brilliant. I especially admire *Memento*, which, as I'm sure you know (right?) is told in this weird amnesiac backward fashion. Starring the kind of hottie who makes bleach-blond hair on a guy seem like not just an interesting choice but an important one, *Memento* isn't as tightly put together as you think it is, as you'll see if you watch it thirty-one times—but then: The Nolan brothers got me to watch it thirty-one times, so who am I to critique.

The Wachowskis! The Wachowski siblings are very awesome. They grew up super working class, one of them came out as transgender, which is amazing and brave, and after the *Matrix* films, their *Cloud Atlas* was almost viciously underrated. If I were the type to cry in movie theaters, I would have cried, because the *sheer ambition* of how they pulled off *Cloud Atlas*—the most expensive independent film of all time—is astonishing. Great soundtrack, too. Oof, the visuals. You *have* to put it on the list.

Even the Farrelly brothers, of ridiculous old Cameron Diaz comedies, of the *Dumb and Dumber* franchise, which is a frightening concept on every level, even *they* had each other.

You know what none of the above filmmakers had? A sibling who took off, mid-oeuvre.

In the old days Annabeth and I used to ride our bikes to the Liberty Movie House in Mount Lebanon on Sundays, even though it was on this slightly sketchy strip. The Liberty used to be flat-out majestic, and if you blur your focus, it still is. There are stars painted into the ceiling. There is an Arabian setting painted onto the walls. A popcorn and a Coke is four dollars, *total*, and I guess some local donor keeps the place going because he's a huge and reclusive old movie buff and supposedly lives in like Pittsburgh's version of a "mansion."

"Where's my birthday boy off to?" Mom says, discovering me as I'm reaching for the door to the garage.

"I think I'm gonna ride to Mount Lebo and see what's playing at the Liberty."

"Should you look up showtimes first?" Mom says. She shifts on her feet, uneasy. Mom's from the generation of people who believe that no event can occur unless they've seen it listed in the paper first.

"Nah, I like to be surprised." I give her a quick peck. "Especially on my birthday!"

I disappear into the garage, to the land of humid exhaust. It's the weirdest thing. We haven't had a car parked here for, oh, exactly six months now. And yet it still reeks of exhaust. Maybe this is how Annabeth is haunting us: through clouds of hot gasoline.

"Will you be home in time for supper?" Mom's holding the door open, not quite letting me go. "I thought I might cook you something for your birthday. Something special."

I hit the garage button so that the extremely noisy retracting door drowns out and minimizes the impact of my bad news. Of my lie. "Aw, Ma, Geoff is taking me out for my birthday."

"Tonight, he is?" she says.

"Yeah. Yep."

If I were Pinocchio, my nose would have poked out Mom's eye by now.

She steps into the garage. The overhead door is still opening and it's louder than ever. A dad would, like, WD-40 it or something.

"Here," Mom says, handing me another twenty and shouting over the screeching machinery. I hate to make her shout. "I keep finding money in Grandpa's old stuff."

"What's this for?" I say, trying to play sweet.

"There's a pharmacy on Washington Road, past the post office and before the Presbyterian church that is a mockery of its former self." Mom hates to see a religious institution fall on hard times.

The garage door is finally open. The only sound now is us.

"The pharmacy," Mom continues, "has a whole section in the back, with beauty products."

This is nice. She wants me to buy her some stuff for a makeover, like Annabeth used to do on her.

But no. "Pick up some new cologne before your big dinner thing tonight," Mom says, and her eyes dart away and then she does.

CHAPTER TWENTY-TWO

EXT. LIBERTY THEATER - DAY

Quinn stands on the street outside the theater.

His bright white teeth shine and then seem to
blink, and we see why: The Liberty's exterior
is decorated like the 1940s movie house it is,
the best kind of old-fashioned that feels not
old but instead timeless. The colorful lights
reflect off Quinn's teeth.

He steps up to the ticket taker, an ancient
man, ED (picture your favorite grandpa), whose
back is hunched but whose eyes twinkle like the
Liberty sign above.

                    QUINN

          Ed, my man!

                    ED

          Quinn, my boy. It's been ages!
          Where's that freckly little
          sister of yours?

Quinn's smile somehow doesn't fade. He remains
brave for Ed.

                    QUINN

          Ah, she's actually my *big*
          sister, Ed. And she's not here
          anymore.

Ed looks confused, the way Quinn's mom does
when he tries to explain how to erase stuff on
the DVR.

                    ED

          She went off to college?

                    QUINN

          No, no, that would have been

next year. I mean: she died,

Ed. Annabeth's no longer with

us.

Ed exits the ticket booth, walks slowly around,
and gives Quinn a paternal hug. He is in a very
heavy sweater, despite the summer heat. When
he pulls away, neither guy is crying. They are
both strong.

                    ED

    Stay here.

                  QUINN

    Where are you going?

                    ED

    To talk to the projectionist.

Ed walks with great determination toward the
wide double doors, edged in beautiful brass
buttons, that lead into the Liberty lobby.

                  QUINN

    What for?

                    ED

          Today only, back to back:
          Forrest Gump, then *The
          Wizard of Oz*, then *E.T.*, if
          I've still got it in the
          back.

Quinn looks up at the marquee and laughs.

                  QUINN

          But it says you're playing
          The Poseidon Adventure,
          Eddie.

                    ED

          Not today we're not.

Ed's eyes water. Now he's not strong. It's
beautiful.

                ED (CONT'D)
          Today we're only playing her
          favorites.

Quinn gets choked up. He coughs into his hand.

                              ED (CONT'D)
              And little brothers get in
              free.

He holds the door open for Quinn.

I hope Ed's working today. He's so grumpy and sweet. Old
guys are the best. I hope I get really old and wear scratchy
sweaters and treat obviously gay kids like they're extra special.

It's been a while since I've been to Mount Lebo, and when
I cross the street, I don't even bother locking up my bike,
because who the hell is going to steal a Mongoose on a Sunday?

Maybe I'm feeling overly optimistic about the forty new
bucks in my pocket, or about the day of movies ahead before
Amir's temporarily-going-away party tonight, and I guess what
I'm saying is: I'm feeling so good, I catch myself off guard when
I hear the word "No" before realizing it's me who's saying it.

Ed is not working at the Liberty. The Liberty is not even
open. There's a big sign placed over one of its beautiful old window cards, which once displayed vintage movie posters and now
has these giant red letters: FOR RENT, CONTACT JENNIFER "JEN"
RICHART AT RICHART REALTY. And I'm thinking two things:

1) No, this cannot be fucking happening.

2) Jennifer "Jen" Richart, way to go with the highly original nickname.

I'm standing and staring and staring, and my raspberry iced tea is working its way like a chemical-fueled speeding train toward my bladder, and finally a homeless man, who is lounging in the shade of the marble entrance of the theater, goes, "Bummer, right?"

He's the kind of bum where he probably actually had really good parents who wanted big things for him and he's slowly making his way across the country till he can live in Portland or whatever. What I'm saying is, he's not far gone. He's actually kind of cute, if you squint, which I am, because it's sunny and I always lose sunglasses.

"Is it like *closed*-closed?" I say.

"Yeah, like, six months ago."

"What happened?"

The homeless man sits up. I like his shirt, like, a lot. This is my life.

"The old dude died."

"Ed?" I say stupidly.

"Don't know names, bro. It was the guy who, like, funded the theater."

You can't ask a crazy person to explain anything, and so don't ask me why I'm tearing down "Jen" Richart's real estate sign, but I am. As if by pulling it down, the lights will flicker back on, Ed will take my ticket, I'll have a place to pee, and be.

"Of course," I say when I see it. The ad for the last movie that played here. "*The Wizard of Oz*," I say out loud, for the homeless man or maybe for myself. Or for my sister. Her second-favorite movie of all time, after *E. T.*—"The best movie ever, shut up shut up shut up," she'd say, when I'd make fun of her for such an obvious choice. But you know what? She was right. Her favorite films—*Forrest Gump* and *E. T.* and *The Wizard of Oz*—were sappy and sincere and actually not quite perfect, and so was she.

"We're not in Kansas anymore, Toto," the guy says. He chuckles and leans back, and the crazy person being played by me goes, "That's not the line; everyone gets that line wrong." The *correct* version of the quote is in my top-ten favorite movie quotes, in fact.

I take a step toward him. I lean my hand against the box office glass and realize its windows are now wholly papered with flyers for moving companies and babysitters and lost cats. I begin tearing them all down.

"Chill your harsh, bro."

"It's just, if you're going to quote a famous line, you know, get it right," I mutter, but I guess loudly enough to piss the guy off. And so when he gets up and starts toward me, I think he's going to lunge or something, but he doesn't. He just smiles a little and juts his chin out, as if using it as a pointer.

"I believe somebody is making off with your bike, Toto," he says. He has perfect teeth. I was definitely right: His parents had big plans for him.

I turn around. Two kids half my size have found a way to

board my little Mongoose, together, like a circus act, and are jamming away with it down the street.

I drop all the paper advertisements and take off after the little punks. Just as I make it out of the frame—tripping past the Quiznos that has the best raspberry iced tea and feeling my stomach gurgle—one of the flyers, advertising a candlelight vigil for a local girl killed in a car accident six months back, gets swept up in a manufactured breeze that has been added by a set decorator simply so that this sequence ends with a visual flourish. The flyer blows directly into the screen of the camera, cutting to the next scene.

CHAPTER TWENTY-THREE

QUINN ROBERTS'S TOP-TEN MOVIE QUOTES

1. "A boy's best friend is his mother." (*Psycho*, 1960)

2. "As God is my witness, I'll never be hungry again." (*Gone with the Wind*, 1939)

3. "Fasten your seat belts. It's going to be a bumpy night." (*All About Eve*, 1950)

4. "I coulda been a contender." (*On the Waterfront*, 1954)

5. "Keep your friends close, but your enemies closer." (*The Godfather: Part II*, 1974)

6. "I'll be right here." (*E.T.*, 1982)

7. "Toto, I've a feeling we're not in Kansas anymore." (*The Wizard of Oz*, 1939)

8. "We'll always have Paris." (*Casablanca*, 1942)

9. "What we've got here is failure to communicate." (*Cool Hand Luke*, 1967)

You'll notice there's no tenth. I'm still waiting to happen upon it. I suppose that's just the kind of guy I am: whimsical.

CHAPTER TWENTY-FOUR

It's an amazing thing when two prepubescent kids on a Mongoose bicycle built for one can outspeed a full-grown nearly adult teenager, but there you have it. I'm stuck in Mount Lebanon without a ride home, without a movie to see, with too many hours to worry myself into the over-written version of what tonight's going-away party for Amir is going to be like. I'm not ready for him to leave. He just arrived.

"My, people come and go so quickly here." (*The Wizard of Oz*, 1939)

I'd get out my new phone to text Geoff to come pick me up, but the contacts aren't synced yet and the only number I have memorized is my mom's landline, which hasn't been connected for months. So when I stomp past the old Presbyterian church, I figure I may as well make the most of my misery and stop into the family-run drugstore to pick up some new cologne. Mom's gift to me.

Look at me. Attempting optimism again. Twice in one week, new world record.

I'm in the beauty section thinking maybe this will be the summer I bring CK One back, when: "Mr. Roberts," I hear, and I'd know that voice anywhere.

"Whaddup, Mrs. Kelly."

So. Weird. She's wearing pristine white sneakers and a T-shirt, and I can barely wrap my head around seeing this totally buttoned-up Republican anywhere but in her cinder-block counselor's office at school, grilling me.

"Well, here we are," she says. In a screenplay, we sometimes write in "(beat)" when we want an actor to take a purposeful pause. Imagine a lot of (beats) here, because, *finally*, she goes: "You look fantastic, Mr. Roberts."

"Oh, thanks," I say. "You, uh, look the exact same. You haven't changed!"

"I've been working my tail off at the gym." Mrs. Kelly tucks a strand of hair behind her ear. "I've lost maybe twenty pounds since the last time I saw you."

"Oh, *jeez*," I say. "I was kidding, Mrs. Kelly. You look amazing."

"Please, Mr. Roberts." If an entire face could do an eye roll, hers does. "I've been married twice. I know when a man is lying."

Mrs. Kelly is holding some kind of nutrition powder in a bulk container, and the weight of it seems to be making her arms shake. What kind of gym could she possibly be going to if it hasn't prepared her for the weight of a jar of powder?

"Can I help you with that?" I say, and I put the CK One down and she hands the powder to me, and, with no discernible segue, goes: "There's still time, you know. I haven't legally been allowed to reach out directly, but as your counselor, I am as committed to getting you into a good college as I am the next studen—"

"Thanks, Mrs. Kelly. Let's see what happens," I say. I've never liked school. Nobody in my family has ever finished college. Why upset the applecart? "I've been looking into getting my GED, and I was thinking about getting a job, so stuff is *def*initely on the horizon."

Mrs. Kelly bypasses my words. "Have you gotten any of the packets I had your teachers send home? You really *can* start senior year right on track."

I keep picturing what it would feel like to drive past The Pug every day, to pull past Annabeth's dog face and see the school flagpole, which will, no doubt, be permanently at half-mast, as a tribute. Kill me now. As if homeroom wasn't tragic enough already.

My phone rings. No idea who it is, but it's local.

"I should get this," I say, handing back the protein powder, which was, by the way, heavy as fuck. My bad! "It's an important call."

Where is her mean face? Where is Mrs. Kelly's judginess? She is being so kind and patient. She is frustrating me. "Of course," she says.

I step away and swipe to talk.

"Hey," I hear.

"G., hey, you have my new number! Cool."

"Yeah, I *got* you the friggin phone," Geoff goes. "I had to pretend I was you at the Verizon stor—"

"Are you coming with me to Amir's party tonight?"

He sighs. "Uh, no. Just to remind you, he and I aren't really friends. He was just using me to get you cakes and love notes."

"Okay, so what's up?"

"Let's meet up," Geoff says. "In person. I have to . . . show you something."

"Something bad?"

"No." He does this weird pause. Like, a suspicious (beat). "No, I don't think so."

"Okay," I say. "Can you pick me up on Washington Road in Mount Lebo, actually? I got here and then some kids stole my bike."

"Quinn, your life story is starting to turn into a documentary that people would walk out of because it's both too sad and too slow."

Fuck you, I start to say, but I realize Mrs. Kelly is only an aisle over, and suddenly I want her to like me.

"*Well*, then," I say, instead. "Can you show me this mysterious whatever *tonight*? Like, after Amir's party."

"Fine," Geoff says, and just when I'm about to say, *And can you mayyyybe pick me up from Station Square, late?* he goes, "Figure out a way to get to my house," and hangs up.

I check the time on my new phone and realize I should put some work into making myself as hot as possible for later. I feel an incoming-missile zit situation coming on.

"Mrs. Kelly," I say, walking too fast down the aisle and nearly running right into her. She's been spying on me, I think, hiding behind a tower of sympathy cards, but I don't care. In fact, I like it. I feel cared for. "Can you give me a ride home?"

Mom is in the sunroom. She's hugging a pair of Mickey Mouse ears, teeny-tiny Mickey Mouse ears that Annabeth got on our one family road trip to Florida. I can tell Mom's been sorting through everything—the house is even more turned over than ever, with piles of newspapers and old *Life* magazines pulled up from the basement—and she's asleep and lightly snoring, which is normal. But she's doing something else, at the same time, something headline-making big: LOCAL WOMAN FOUND SMILING FOR LONGER THAN THREE SECONDS IN A ROW. CLICK FOR VIDEO.

I look to the counter. The postcard advertising men's haircuts is gone. She started going through the mail, finally, like some kind of grown-up. Sometimes it's hard to not think of Mom as a kid, herself. Technically speaking, she's an orphan now. And she isn't married. I'm kind of the only thing left that makes her seem like an adult, by default.

One of the lights flickers off in the kitchen. I hope she pays the bill soon.

CHAPTER TWENTY-FIVE

We have this local train thing called "the T" in Pittsburgh. It's our rickety "mass transit system" and our version of an above-ground subway. Everywhere else in my life, I like complete control. But whenever I'm on mass transportation—the T, like tonight, or an airplane, *once*, to Charleston, for a choir trip—I'm actually okay with giving over. With letting the pilot steer. I don't know why.

For the record, the best train scenes of all time are: *Indiana Jones and the Last Crusade* (1989), *The Bridge on the River Kwai* (1957), and, duh, *Strangers on a Train* (1951). I'm not looking these up, by the way. I just know the dates. Can you imagine if I could apply this kind of memory to something genuinely useful?

The Sunday-night T schedule is usually unpredictable, but tonight we're going particularly slow, and I really can't be late to

Amir's party. Apparently it's on a riverboat, and we're traversing one (or all?) of Pittsburgh's three rivers, and it's a whole thing. I only know I have to be there by "seven p.m., sharp," according to his voice mail, which I've listened to so many times that I have started taking the little breaths that he takes, along with him, when I relisten.

"*Ladies and gentlemen,*" I hear from a speaker mounted directly behind my head—making me hop out of my seat and nearly smash into some lady's granny cart, "*because of an incident near Station Square, the T will stop before the tunnels, with free shuttle buses directly to Station Square. This will cause an approximately ten-minute delay in schedule.*"

Well, this is ridiculous, and I'm about to say as much to the other passengers when this guy in full Pirates regalia goes, "This fucking blows," and starts kicking at the doors of the train car. He's really quite violent about it—you can see actual dents forming in the metal—and now he's talking to the granny whose cart I bumped into and trying to loop her into his anger. And as I'm watching him, I realize I don't want to be that kind of guy. The one who ropes people into his fury.

The one who makes fun of his wife's cooking for how it always disappoints him.

The one who never watches a single one of his kids' five-minute-long movies.

I don't want to be that guy.

"This is our last and final stop. Please board the shuttle across the street."

And so I choose not to be.

"Does anyone know where Amir is?" I say, pacing around the launching dock off Station Square, right at the edge of the river. Pittsburgh is so pretty. People think it's not going to be and then it is.

"I don't think he's here yet," someone says. I'm looking and looking for Carly, hoping to see a familiar face, when a girl in a skirt goes, "Pepé Le Pew!" and I realize she and I were on the team of non-natives in the Celebrity game of doom.

"Oh, hey," I go.

"Cool glasses," she says, and I touch them like I'm Cinderella, like my fairy godmother put them on for me. Which I guess she did.

A horn from behind me *honk-honks*, followed by the half-hearted cheers of a group of people trying to look cool. There's so little that people get openly worked up about. A few folks stub out their clove cigarettes, and I see one guy swig from a Dr Pepper in a brown paper bag, and then a faceless voice calls out: *"All aboard!"*

It's him, Amir, jumping out of the back of somebody's car and holding Carly's hand. It makes my stomach shimmy, see-ing them touching each other, and I like that—that I feel pro-tective about a guy, for once. Usually I'm the only guy I feel protective about, ha.

I try to get Amir's attention, but he and Carly run ahead, onto this old-fashioned riverboat called *The Good Ship Lollipop*. A line forms after them, to get on too. These three girls in front of me are guffawing at something on one of their phones, and when I turn away from them, that's when I notice giant floodlights—the kind in stadiums, but also the kind used on film sets. The kind you'd set up if you were shooting a movie on a Sunday night that disrupts the flow of the T, which causes a kid to decide to not react like his dad would, and to hop on a shuttle bus to a going-away party for a boy he was just, well, getting going *with*.

My phone buzzes. "Go to the upper deck, mister," the text says. "I'll find you ☺"

Already, the floodlights are making me dizzy.

CHAPTER TWENTY-SIX

Pittsburgh routinely falls into the top-ten list of places you should live. Fun fact: I haven't visited many places, but Pittsburgh is my favorite city regardless. It's in my blood. I've never been west of Ohio, but someday I want to go to Chicago, maybe. I hear it's like a big Pittsburgh with better pizza, and the lake there is like a small ocean without sharks, which sounds perfect.

"It's, like, so nice up here," some girl says, leaning over the railing on the upper deck of this overcrowded riverboat. And it is nice. I just wish Amir would find me before I'm forced to make small talk with some rando.

At least the captain of the boat tonight has us going at a full clip, which feels like *some*thing. Every time we go beneath a bridge, the captain idles the engine and everyone on the boat lets out a giant cheer, and our voices multiply like bats flapping around in a cave.

I pull out my new phone and debate text options to Amir:

"On the roof with an amir-size hole in my conversation"

Just: "On roof . . ."

and

"If u find me and bring me a drink I will act responsible!!"

The last option makes me smile, and as I'm typing it out, I feel hot beer breath on my face, and look up, and let out a tiny shout, and then I go: "Hey."

"Happy," Amir says, with this weird little break in the sentiment, "birthday." He looks really good. "Thanks for getting down here tonight! Was it a hassle?"

"No. Easiest thing ever."

Someone brings Amir a drink and he says thanks, but when she turns away, he pours half of it over the side of the ship.

"Uh." I laugh. "Why are you doing that?"

"People give you so much crap if you don't get shit-faced," he says. "So I just keep pouring half of it out. I feel responsible for everyone's safety tonight."

He hiccups. He is, actually, a tiny bit drunk. Did everyone arrive at the boat pre-liquored? Is that a thing?

"Did I make a total jagoff of myself last night?" I say. I'm looking at Amir's cup and rather than coveting it, my stomach is playing pinball.

"Naw. You were sweet," he says. Great. "Sweet" is how you describe a toddler. He goes to touch my hair, but the boat hits a wake and he stumbles a little, and so to cover for the awkward moment, I change the camera angle on our conversation.

"Ooh, there goes the Incline," I say, pointing behind Amir.

We have this really cool train that climbs the side of the mountain in Pittsburgh, up to this restaurant called Le Mont, which means "the mountain" in French, and it's fancy (you have to wear a sports coat), and Geoff's parents treated me and Annabeth to dinner there once and we didn't know what to do with all those forks.

"Aw, man, I'm gonna miss Pittsburgh." Close-up, back to Amir.

"Well, how long is your writing program thing?"

Amir puts his hand on my waist and it feels wonderful.

"Do you remember what I said last night, after we bowled, about my, um, going away?"

Oh, boy. I could fake this, but my timing is off. In my mind, I was going to stand here and reenact a whole funny Le Mont montage—about how Annabeth and I used the forks to brush our hair, like Ariel in *The Little Mermaid*—and so I'm caught too off guard to lie.

"Only kind of," I say.

Amir sits us down on an ancient bench whose wood gives almost as much as a pool floaty would. *The Good Ship Lollipop* is like half an iceberg away from disaster.

"Uh, so I'm not sure I'm coming back to Pitt in the fall," Amir says.

Yeah, I definitely don't remember him saying that, because

I'm standing up again, and chugging my 7UP down, fast, and I'm not liking this one bit.

"Where are you going, then, instead?" I say. I put my foot up on the bench, like I'm posing for a Dockers ad. Idiot.

"I got into this pre-MBA business program back at U.T.," he says, running his fingers around the rim of his red plastic cup. "It's a good opportunity. I mean, it would shut my parents up, at least. They sort of threatened not to keep paying for Pitt, so."

"Do you *want* to go into business?" I say.

"No, but I'm feeling a little driftless in Pittsburgh, and a *lot* of my friends are in the program at U.T. By the way, I like your cologne. CK One?"

You have me, I want to say. I know we are good for each other. "You mean *aimless*," I say, and he gets up and places his hand on my knee and goes: "What?" And I say: "*Driftless* is not a word," and Amir chuckles and says, "I don't understand how you're not a good student! You're smarter than me."

"Than *I am*," I say, and we laugh, but I'm not really laughing. I'm panic-flirting, convincing him with little sonic eye-rays to stay here. To stay in Pittsburgh and teach me things and keep telling me I'm smart, I'm smart, I'm smart, until I believe it enough to get out of bed even on days when I have nowhere to go and nobody to collaborate with.

The song of the summer comes on over a jerry-rigged speaker system. Amir skids his hand over my buzz cut and it makes me shiver. I want to ask him what he sees in me. *Why are you even hanging with me at all?* I'd like to say—but somehow the letters switch themselves around, the little rascals, and all I manage to get out is: "Was this boat expensive to rent, or what?"

He makes an offended face, but I stand my ground. "I mean, it's not cheap," he goes, "but it's fine. It's no biggie."

"Okay," I say, pulling my knee away from his hand and feeling antsy. "It just seems like a really big thing to be doing. To, like, rent a boat to give yourself a going-away party when you haven't even been in my hometown a full year."

"Wow, all right. I mean: I made good friends. I wanted to send everyone off in a big way."

"Could you say the first and last names of everyone who's on this boat right now?" I know he can't. I know it.

Amir fake-laughs and puts his drink down on the bench.

"*You* threw up on my shoe last night, mister," he says. I look down. He's got these bright cream-colored Adidas on, and indeed: There is a tan stain across the toe and bleeding into the shoelaces, like the fallout from a dropped casserole.

"Whoa, I'm so sorry," I say.

"It's okay."

I guess Amir is a good starter guy. Throw up on him, try out some theories, say goodbye. Except I don't want to even wave goodbye.

"Have you ever dated somebody as young as me?" I say, and

Amir goes: "Oh, are we *dating*?" and I go, "Oh, no, I mean, I didn't mean that, I just meant: theoretically."

He goes: "No. All of my boyfriends have been a *lot* older," and I'm thinking *All?* when he adds: "And if I dated anyone younger than you"—as he takes my 7UP and puts it on the bench—"I'd have to get paid babysitting money." I instinctively lunge for the cup, and when I come back up with it, Amir takes my chin, with this wonderful kind of too much force, and brings my lips to his.

This isn't how I wrote our first kiss. And yet.

His tongue is inside my mouth, and it is simultaneously bigger and wetter and also more delicious than anything I've ever eaten. I can *taste* him, I mean, and our teeth bump, and I'm not sure if I'm doing it wrong, but when he laughs, I know it's not a mean laugh.

"A little less tongue," he slurs, which was precisely the note I was going to give to him. When we go at it again, I'm giving him, like, no tongue, and he pulls away and goes, "The hottest thing about *you* is you don't know how hot you even *are* yet." He pulls my waist in to his, and the song cuts out, and somebody goes, *"Look!"*

A riot of fireworks launch into the night sky, lighting up Amir's glasses in confetti-green bursts. It's not the Fourth of July, because my birthday is in June and goddammit, it's still my birthday, and for one brief, odd moment, I consider whether Amir ordered fireworks for me or maybe for himself.

Burst. Burst. Burst. The sky is trying to break apart. We both look up.

"Did you, wait, like, *arrange* these for my birthday?" I ask. The Hot Metal Bridge, which we're idling under, looks rusted to oblivion. Like it could collapse on us. And so suddenly I want to get away, out from underneath this dare.

"*Win,*" Amir goes.

"Yeah?"

"I said no, I don't know why fireworks are going off. Maybe for some sports thing?"

But nothing's playing tonight. If a game were playing tonight, the T would have been littered with more angry people just like that guy I don't want to be.

Now the night clouds are red, and now they're purple, and now they're yellow, and yet the giant kaleidoscope sky feels smaller, somehow, than Amir's tongue in my mouth, which is happening again—smaller than the fact that his mustache zone is scratchy enough to be making my lip burn.

"Can I say something risky?" Amir says, pulling away and hiding a hiccup, and I go, "Anything," quick and quiet, and he goes, "I think we need to get you laid tonight."

And now the sky is yellow, yellow, white, white, white, the finale, bombs bursting in air like something not quite patriotic but rather peculiarly crass. My choir trip to Charleston coincided with some national holiday, and when we landed at the Pittsburgh International Airport, it was nighttime, and as we descended through the clouds, we saw about twenty different displays of fireworks happening across all the flat regions and towns that dot Pittsburgh's edges. I was the only person on the plane from Charleston that night who wasn't in awe of the fireworks but rather was thinking: 1) I hope we don't get *hit* by a stray firework; and 2) If I survive this plane ride, I need to remember this imagery so that someday I can use this scene in a screenplay.

"So I guess that's a *no*," Amir says, "about getting you laid."

He throws his head back to "drink" from his red cup, but I know he finished it more than ten minutes ago. I know because I saw him chug the rest of it. I am distracted by seeing *everything*, and so instead of telling him that getting laid tonight sounds negotiable, possible, probable even—the most unique seventeenth birthday present a guy could want—I'm suddenly watching Carly, who's woozily trying to keep her cool as she approaches Amir from behind.

"*Meer,*" she says, salty like he's been ignoring her all night. "The captain-dude-guy wants to know if you want to head back now, or in ten minutes."

Amir swings around. "What are you talking about? I rented this thing for like a whole nother hour."

Carly juts her pointer finger into his shoulder. Beer sloshes against the sides of her cup, like when you cannonball into a hot tub. "Don't shoot the *mesh*-enger," she says, her inebriated sentences turning all-vowel before our very eyes.

The engine below revs back up. The boat begins a creaky

turn back toward those weird floodlights at shore. Amir looks at me and goes, "Stay here," and then gets close and whispers, "*and cut Carly off*," and when he's gone to the lower deck, my arms get pin-prickled with wet river air. In the hazy firecracker smoke, Carly almost looks like Geoff.

"Hey," I go, "do you know why your brother is pissed at me?"

"For*get* him," Carly goes. "Let's talk about Quinn and *Amiiir*, huh?"

As if he and I have formed a law firm.

"How is Amir even *affording* all of this?"

"Oh, baby," Carly says, adjusting a bra strap and smacking her gum. "His dad is like megabucks."

"Oh, no shit?"

"Yup. I *basically* set you up with a prince."

"Wait, literally?"

Carly scrunches her eyebrows and shouts, to top the rainbow-colored rockets above: "No, Q. Not *literally*-literally."

"Oh."

"Anyway, even princes are human. He had his heart broken this year." (beat) "Be gentle with him."

I lean in. "*Actually*, Carly?" I say, making her play my older sister in a surprise moment of stunt casting: "I think Amir wants to have s-e-x tonight."

Literally I spell it out. If I say the actual word, I'll be one inch closer to it, and it intimidates me.

"Wait, this is *amazing*," Carly says, dancing in a little circle, which seems to dip her even deeper into the well of drunk. "That is, like, an *opportunity*, Quinn!" Loud. Too loud. "Amir is, like, *experienced.*"

I try to blink away the most recent firecracker. "Well, we'll see."

"Don't 'we'll see' me, kiddo. Is he not the hottest? Did *I* not set you up with the hottest?"

"He's hot, yeah."

"The hottest. Don't let me down, Quinn."

Wow, I was actually kind of hoping she'd back me up here; tell me to wait until I feel ready. How do guys even *have* sex together? I mean, I've seen the videos, but how does it not, like, *hurt*? Sorry, serious question.

I lean my hip against the railing, right into my bruise from the bowling alley table. "Carly, you brokering my virginity is kind of freaking me out, to be honest."

"Quinny, I just want you to *live* a little."

I look back at the Incline, wishing I were on it.

"I dunno," I say—and then I pull out my secret weapon, my magic trick, the ace to beat all hands: "The whole situation makes me feel guilty. You know, 'cause Annabeth never got to kiss anyone."

Carly says, "O . . . *kay*," into her beer, like she and the foam are in on a secret, and I pull the cup away from her lips and over Carly's "Hey" I say, *"What?"* thinking she's being funny or something. Thinking, I dunno, maybe Carly and my sister practiced kissing on each other once.

"Nothing, *nothing*," Carly goes, doing a tipsy thing my dad used to do where he'd have a secret but he wouldn't give it up until you begged.

"You're being an ass," I say, and I drop my 7UP cup between my feet and try to kick it around to look cool. But: "Okay, *fine*. I'll bite. What are you not telling m—"

"It's *not* my place to say, Quinny," Carly says, reaching forward to do something with my collar. I smack her hand away, too hard, and feel horrible about it, but she doesn't even register it. Her eyes are now fully fogged over with beer, and so I make like a lighthouse. A lighthouse never sways.

"Not your place to say *what*, Car—"

"I just think you've got this image of your sister as a *nun*, but she was a *fun* girl, Q. I just don't think Annabeth was like an all-time *saint*."

"I'm not *saying* she was a saint, but she *was* a virgin, and that fact isn't going to change anytime soon."

Carly gulps back one more swig of beer and comes up for air. "Yeah, well, you might want to check in with Geoff about that."

The fireworks stop. Amir's head appears from the stairwell downstairs, and he goes to call something irrelevant to us, but I don't let him.

"What did you just fucking say?" I say. I touch Carly's chin, just like Amir did with me, but God knows I'm not going to kiss her. "What did you just say? Is that some kind of *joke*?" I knock Carly's cup out of her hands.

Now Amir's standing between us like Lou Fillipo, the bow-tied ref in *Rocky*. "Uh, *guys*? What's going on here?"

That's when the fireworks start up again, right back to the same colors as the beginning, an entirely repeat show. Amir ducks down and covers his ears, but Carly looks right at me and says, with a frightening kind of clarity that only the truly drunk can summon: "Geoff and I had a bet going. I honestly thought you knew."

"Knew *what*, Carly?"

"That he and your sister were a thing."

were a thing

were a thin

were a thi

"I think that's enough," Amir says, but I'm already stepping on both of our red cups, and crushing them. Then I push past Amir and Carly, and I slip down the wet steps and twist my ankle, but I immediately find the captain, who is hanging out with a couple of sorority girls, and I say: "Amir wants you to take us back to Station Square now." My voice is shaking, and I am, and the captain goes: "He just said he wanted another forty-five minutes, kid," but I say louder than the fireworks: "He changed his fucking mind."

CHAPTER TWENTY-SEVEN

EXT. STATION SQUARE - NIGHT

Quinn stands in a line of people at the boat
dock, waiting to board the shuttle bus back to
the South Hills.

The fireworks continue to explode overhead, and
the crowd around Quinn is admiring the sky,
taking selfies, but Quinn is lost in his own
world.

CUT TO:

INT. SHUTTLE BUS TO THE T - NIGHT

Quinn is now on his phone, on the shuttle bus,
reinstating all of his social networking apps:
scrolling past months of well-wishing and
rainbow pictures and smiley faces and frowny
faces, back to before.

                    QUINN
        Aha.

He lands on one of Annabeth's posts, at the
beginning of December, before she was killed.
He is looking for clues: when were she and
Geoff seeing each other?

How did Quinn not know? How could the two
closest people to him have been carrying on
such a secret and secretive backstory without
Quinn's knowledge?

How. How could they not have told me?
"Move up, dude," somebody says. I'm still in Station
Square, in line for the shuttle back through the tunnel and
to the T, so that we can all go back south. No—so that I can
go to Geoff's house and bash his face in. I will figure out the
theory of why my anger at him is white hot like a griddle
sometime between Beechview and Keystone Oaks.

"What the actual fuck is up with these fireworks?" I say to the guy behind me.

"They're shooting some movie."

And that is all he has to say.

As if perched on stilts that have a brain of their own, my legs walk me away from the shuttle bus, which is expelling a black smog that coughs and hiccups like Carly back on the boat of secrets. My stilts are taking me to this temporary chain-link fence that I now realize isn't typically found in Station Square, which is a sort of upscale mall place.

There are handsome, fit men all around, who don't look as if they're from Pittsburgh, standing at a kind of gated entrance into a massive area where the Summer Jam series offers concerts that Mom never lets me come downtown for. But there's no band playing tonight.

Tonight the temporary floodlights spill over and practically compete with the fireworks above, and I see a giant movie camera high in the sky, and a woman looking into the monitor, and she yells, *"Cut!"* Not twelve seconds later the fireworks stop and some background extras clap.

I know what this is.

"Hey, I am—I'm with *South Hills Apprentice*," I blurt out to a guy with a clipboard and a walkie-talkie. He holds his finger up to me and says into a little mouthpiece, "Yeah, we're going back for one more take. Have Bryson go to makeup." And then he's with me, kind of. "What did you say?"

"I'm with *South Hills Apprentice*," I say, certain I'm getting this right. This has to be it. I know it is.

"And you are?"

"Quinn Roberts. I'm with Ricky Devlin's entourage."

Lies spill from my mouth as fully formed sitcom pilots.

The camera behind the fence descends and the woman hops off. A P.A. hands her a bottle of water. This lady huddles up a crew next, and I am immediately as enamored of the shooting of *South Hills Apprentice* as I have been with any film ever.

I want to be in this world. I want to get past this guy at the gate and go to craft services and eat free cheese, and get lost.

"Do you have a badge, or what?" the guy says.

"I forgot it in my trailer," I say.

Rookie mistake. I wouldn't have a trailer if I weren't an actor, but one thing Ricky Devlin taught me: Write dialogue fast, fast, fast, because people don't think before they talk. Make it real. Make it true. But it didn't work so much this time.

"Why don't you show me your ID, then, and I can check the master list."

But I know there's no way I'm getting past this guy.

A mosquito lands on his neck and I don't tell him, and I see, behind the fence: the skinny star and the frustrated director having a little fight. "Having words," my mom would say. The actress pulls from a discreet pocket in her skirt a piece of a script—just one page—and they are arguing over dialogue. I know this. I know this because Annabeth would call me when she was shooting our films, to say: *So-and-so feels stupid saying this line*, or, *The weather changed and now it's ridiculous to refer to the sun; can we just say "the clouds,"* and I would tweak and rewrite over the phone, and that is what is happening. I know it. I know this conversation.

"So, you kind of have to get lost," the guy says to me, because—UPDATE—I'm now leeched onto the chain-link, pressing my chin through it. At this moment a new guy arrives onto the scene: too muscular, with hair too long to make up for a bald spot that shines in the floodlight, as if he is lit from within and his lid has come off.

"Ricky Devlin!" I yell, I really do, but he can't hear me. The extras are making so much noise that I want to shush them, but there isn't time, because a strong hand is on my shoulder and peeling me from the fence, just as I'm watching Ricky Devlin get pulled into the director/star conversation, all three of them swarmed by the many bugs that populate a midwestern summer night.

"You're too young for me to call security on you," the guy says, "so let's not make a scene." He looks away from me and nods at someone, and goes, "Go on through," and when I turn, I recognize the someone, but how? He is short, handsome, has a bartender vibe. He has a badge, too. And then: "Juan!" I say. Ricky Devlin's boyfriend looks at me, startled. His lips are big and I see immediately the appeal they'd have.

"Do I know y—?"

"Tell Ricky Devlin that Quinny Roberts is here and is desperate to see him."

The man with the hand is saying, "Security to gate two" quietly into his radio thingy, but Juan puts his palm up and goes, "Quinn Roberts," and I say, "Quinn Roberts," and Juan goes: "This kid's with me" to the man with the hand, who backs down and seems sad to have to let go of his small window of control.

I am brought through the gates to Ricky Devlin.

"Rick," Juan says, "you're not going to believe who I found."

Apparently I've been spoken of.

But Ricky Devlin doesn't care who Juan found, because Ricky is squatting down with an old-school pencil—he always wrote first drafts with a pencil—and rewriting something. He has moved out of the glare of the floodlight and knelt next to a drinks cooler, with a firefly hovering over his shoulder as if to light the page.

"*Rick*," Juan says again. "It's your first fan."

Ricky Devlin finally glances up and goes, "Not now, Juani," but Juan literally pushes me forward, and *now* Ricky Devlin looks at me, hard, like I'm a ten-minute timed essay that he doesn't know how to start, and I go: "It's me, Ricky Devlin."

Perhaps nobody has Charlie Browned his name in a long time, because the script page falls from his lap and blows against the chain-link fence, and the actress reaches for it and murmurs these newly-written-on-the-spot lines out loud to the director, and Ricky Devlin doesn't care.

He is up now and gripping my triceps, if I had triceps, and looking as if he might weep.

"These lines are perfect," the skinny star is saying behind him. "It's what I've been asking for all along—finally."

That's when one stray firework goes off in the distance, and nearly hits a passing airplane. But Ricky and I don't flinch.

CHAPTER TWENTY-EIGHT

We are in a makeshift tent and I am eating, eating, eating, so much free stuff you'd think it was my birthday dinner, which, it turns out, it is. You wouldn't believe the amount of free cheese and chips and even burritos and celery and stuff they've got on a real Hollywood film shoot, but they do, my God, they do.

"I was extremely sorry to hear about Annabeth, over Christmas," Ricky Devlin says. He is fiddling with one of the puka-shell necklaces that hot California surfer boys wear. He is too old to be wearing it, but maybe not.

"Yeah, it beyond sucks," I say. I am stuffing myself with carrots. My mouth isn't sure how to react to such subtle flavorings.

"I probably have to get back on set soon," Ricky Devlin says. "Big night. Fourth of July scene." He keeps trying *not* to look at something happening behind me. I'm picturing one of the people in a headset, glaring at Ricky Devlin and pointing to a watch on her wrist, as if to say: Time is money in Hollywood, if not in Pittsburgh. In Pittsburgh, time is just endless. "But you're welcome to hang around tonight, as my guest. I really hope you do."

I push the plate away. There is so much to say and ask, and the truth is, I feel like I've arrived at Ricky Devlin as if he's the mentor in my own hero's journey, so that he'll give me the sword to go and find Geoff and kill him. But that would put me square at the beginning of the film—you always meet the mentor at the beginning—and God knows I have to start wrapping this up.

"Ricky Devlin, I'm lost in my screenplay."

"Whoa! I'm thrilled to hear you're still writing!" he says. He holds up a pointer finger to the person behind me, as if to go: *One more minute with this charity case and I'll be right there.*

"No, I mean: the screenplay of my *life.*" I realize how this sounds. I don't care. It's my fucking birthday. "There's a lot of shit that went down this week. I came out of hibernation. My mom started finding old money from my grandpa. I, like, went to Kennywood."

No, no, no. These aren't the important details. Jesus, Quinn, always cut the prologue.

"I'm not totally following," Ricky Devlin says. His eyes don't twinkle anymore. They used to twinkle.

"I met this really cute *guy* this week," I say.

"Wow!" Ricky goes. "Little Quinny Roberts, all grown up." *Now* he's twinkling. "God, what are you, like, eighteen?" And leaning in. "I can't believe you're this cute *man* now, with, like, a *butt*."

"Uh, no." Weird. Ignore. "I'm seventeen, as of, like, ten hours ago."

(beat) Ricky leans back. (beat) I lean in.

"So . . . anyway, I met this boy and I really *like* him, but I also just found out something *crazy* about my sister and my best friend, and I can't tell if this is the part where 'shit happens' or where I go home 'beaten up but a little wiser.'"

"Oh my God," Ricky goes. "You remember my Hero's Journey screenwriting guide."

"Remember it?" I say. I bounce my knee so hard underneath these makeshift tables that I whack into a metal bar, and it stings. "I use it every day. It's my, like, *life* guide."

"Quinn, I hate to break it to you—"

I hold up *my* finger now. "Then don't." I stop bouncing my knee. "I don't want anything else broken to me. Or on me." There is a buzz of walkie-talkies all around us, and I realize we are being circled. That perhaps half the entire crew is upon us, trying to pull Ricky Devlin from my apparently *Lolita*-like grip. (Interesting film; skip the '97 remake; haven't read the book.)

"I see you people," Ricky Devlin says to them. "Give me another minute." The twinkle is gone again, replaced by two little pinpricks called tired eyes. He looks like an old picture of himself, with a bad filter thrown on top that's giving him not an eternal tan but rather a speckled crust.

"Just help me with, like, one thing," I say to him. "When you get stuck with a scene, do you always go back to the formula?" I reach for my phone. I want to take notes.

Somebody hands Ricky Devlin some big-ass earphones. "You want the truth?"

"Of course," I say.

"This is the fourth screenplay I sold."

"Okay?" I open up the Notes app on my phone. "That's awesome."

"And it's the first one where I threw out all the rules and just wrote from, like, my heart. No rules. No three-act structure. I wrote it on spec in one weekend, and my agents sold it the next Thursday. Fuck the inciting incident. Fuck the page count. Just write the truth."

I can't be hearing this. "Um." This is awful news. Ricky Devlin's screenwriting basics are my Bible. This is . . . a test. *Yes*, this is classic. He is the impostor. He is donning a false mask. Do not trust this.

"Quinny," he says, but I'm moaning a little bit, "I really have to get back to set, which is sort of killing me. But like I said, you can—"

"It's my birthday," I say. I push away from the table and grab his arm. I am a madman.

"That's right," Ricky Devlin says. He touches my hand. "You made us celebrate your entire birthday *week* when I sat for you guys. So funny."

"They're tearing down the Liberty," I say.

"They're—wait, what?"

You sometimes don't remember something until you're standing in front of it. It was Ricky Devlin who introduced me to the Liberty. He cried at *The Shawshank Redemption*. I was embarrassed for him, and then I wasn't.

I pull my hand out from beneath his.

"Yeah, or they're renting it out," I say. "It got shut down. The rich guy who financed the Liberty died."

Ricky Devlin rolls his eyes. "Jesus, I leave this town and the whole thing goes to pot." I'll say this: Ricky Devlin has amazing arms. They are huge, almost quadlike. He was skinny like me when he was closer to my age. Can I have his arms someday, without also having the bald spot? He got to keep his sister, so can I keep my hair?

"I *loved* the Liberty," Ricky Devlin says. He shakes his head in a way that's too over the top, like when your high school counselor pretends to care that your dad left your mom on her fortieth birthday.

A loud bell goes off, a school bell almost. Ricky Devlin stands up and backs away.

"Let me sign something for you, for your birthday."

All this time I had Ricky Devlin pegged as the God figure

who would one day return as a majestic, helpful spirit, with eternally thick hair and eyes that twinkle endlessly. . . .

"Here," he says. He has torn off a corner of a paper. He has signed it for me. "Stick around and stay on the fringes. And keep in touch, Quinny."

"Okay."

But I don't stick around. I watch Ricky Devlin take a glance back at me and bite his lip and then exit the tent, back out to the floodlights, and I look around and steal a few handfuls of soy sauce packets, Mom's favorite condiment, and then open his note, which he folded in half like a Celebrity clue.

"*Happy Birthday to Quinny Roberts, who grew up,*" Ricky's autograph says. "*From your old friend RD.*"

He has gone Hollywood on me.

He has written down his e-mail address and dated the note at the top—and seeing my birthday like that, I realize the six-month anniversary of Annabeth's death is almost here. She and I never missed a half birthday. We grew up in a household that never skipped an opportunity for sweets. A neighbor would die and mom would take us out for sundaes: to celebrate "the life they had," as if she even knew the names of their kids.

As if Amir even knew the names of everyone on his own boat tonight.

I fold up Ricky Devlin's note and slide it into my pocket and head for the exit, and I step right onto the next sputtering shuttle that's leaving for the T. And instead of reinstating all my social networking apps, I power down my new phone and close my eyes and save up my energy to confront a guy I don't even know anymore, who has somehow figured into this particular birthday being the biggest letdown since the 1977 *Exorcist* sequel.

But mostly I'm thinking: Ricky Devlin isn't the golden guy of my past, or even my future. He isn't going to rescue me. I'm on my own here, and maybe I don't see everything after all.

CHAPTER TWENTY-NINE

The scale of my life is all warped.

I'd been in my room for so many months that I've begun to think that humans only need about ten square feet of living space. A twin-size bed, a closet with a broken hinge, a mini-fridge. And so standing here on Geoff's lawn—the greenest lawn in all the land—I can't even imagine what you do with all that space inside. And that's saying something, because I don't even have to.

I grew up in that house.

They kept track of how tall I was growing with little pencil marks in the door frame of their perfect, gleaming kitchen.

His dad taught me how to drive.

His sister used to dress me up in tutus.

The incomplete full-length film that I was eighty-five pages into writing, last fall, would have starred a young boy who wore tutus and army boots and was a superhero in his own mind. An eight-year-old ideally would have played him, the last age you can be without being self-conscious. It's true. Once you hit nine, it's all downhill, because you start noticing things other than the comics and your own belly button, and that sadness of growing subtly older sets in right around when you turn ten, which is why society has created such a big deal out of "double digits."

We make a huge-ass deal out of "double digits" because if we didn't, kids would just start walking into traffic. We trick them into thinking double digits is when the glory years hit.

Incorrect.

Take it from a double-digit virgin.

Last September Annabeth cast a redheaded kid down the block to play the tutu-and-boots-wearing superhero, whose character's code name in the movie, by the way, is "Double Digits," which is also the name of the movie. Our last one together. It was a dark comedy: The kid is part of a society where when you turn double digits, you are sent into battle. It's like a younger *Hunger Games* but doesn't take itself so seriously. God, that film could have used some authentic laughs and not just the kind you get by putting old sitcom stars in funny wigs.

Double Digits was my most ambitious effort, and I had the whole thing plotted out. Or, most of it. I used Ricky Devlin's guide, but I hadn't finished the last fifteen-ish pages of the script, and Annabeth and I fought over that all this past

September and October. She said if I wasn't going to write that college character recommendation for Mrs. Wadsworth to sign, "Can you at *least* finish your *screenplay*?"

We nearly killed each other on every film, even the five-minute jokey ones. I suppose it took an hour-long dark comedy for me to literally murder my sister.

"Jesus Christ, you look like a murderer, standing there."

"Oh," I say, turning to find my potentially former best friend, who's idling next to me at the curb in front of his ginormous house. "Why aren't you inside?"

He rolls his eyes. "Sorry, Quinn, my character can't always be where you want him to be." He pulls into the drive and cuts the engine. "Should we go in?"

"How long were you guys lying to me?" I say, staying put. I want this moment to play out right here on the lawn. "You and me and Annabeth were a club of three," I say. "That was all I had." It comes out stilted. Not even Pacino could pull this junk off.

Geoff's eyes go wide. "Yeah, Carly just texted me about what happened on the boat," he goes. "I'm gonna kill her. Let's not do this out here."

"No, seriously," I say, working myself up. Making a neighbor's dog growl. "When were you going to tell me you were sneaking around with my dead sister?"

"Well, she wasn't exactly dead at the time."

I open Geoff's car door.

EXT. GEOFF'S PERFECT LAWN - NIGHT

Quinn takes Geoff by the lapels and flings him
onto the lawn. He straddles Geoff and digs his
knee right between Geoff's ribs.

> QUINN
> Seriously. Explain yourself so
> that I don't freak out.

> GEOFF
> We didn't want to tell you.
> We were afraid you would
> overreact. Like, you know:
> right now.

I reach for Geoff's lapels, but what kind of kid wears lapels? He's in a T-shirt. His seat belt is still on, and I don't fling him onto the lawn. I simply grab some fabric, and goddammit we both start laughing.

"This isn't funny," I say. I say it again, *"This isn't funny,"* to convince myself, and then I collapse onto the grass and bring my heel down into it, one-two-three, until I hit dirt, and Geoff goes, "At least leave my lawn alone. That thing is my mom's pride and joy," and when I look up at him one tear accidentally falls from my eye like Demi Moore in *Ghost* (massively underrated performance/film), and Geoff goes: "Come on, birthday boy, let's go inside."

So we do. We head to his basement, which is finished within an inch of its life. The whole thing feels like a showroom; you have to take off your shoes and everything.

"When were you going to tell me?" I say, again.

Geoff sits on a sofa that's equally beautiful and uncomfortable.

"We didn't, like, know how to. Seriously. It was like friggin' Romeo and Juliet the way we had to sneak aroun—"

"Oh my God, the fact that you're even referring to the two of you as a 'we.'" I pick up a fake metal apple from a ceramic bowl.

"Dude, we knew you'd freak out. We just, like, instinctively *knew* you wouldn't support us. That you'd be this, like, weird kind of jealous." I go to say, *That's so not fair*, but he keeps barreling on. "You were so tired of Annabeth getting everything handed to her first in life that we were like: If he finds out we're in a relationship before he even comes out of the closet, himself . . ."

I almost throw the apple at his mom's wall. "I wouldn't have been jealous!" I say. "I would have appreciated you being honest with me!"

Geoff's lips sputter. "You're so full of shit, Q."

"Give me *one* example of how I've been *anything* less than a best frien—"

"Sometimes it feels like all you care about is your screen-plays. Or *cared*."

He is hugging a sofa cushion, and when I un-blur my eyes, I realize he is actually using it for protection.

"Yeah, well, I don't think I'm ever getting back to my screenplay. I don't have a reason to."

"That's actually," Geoff says. "This is an awkward segue—but that's why I wanted you to come over tonight." He puts the pillow aside slowly as if setting down a weapon outside a hostage situation. "A package showed up at my house this week. Like, for you. I've been trying to find a way to . . . Just, hold on."

Geoff disappears for a moment into a storage room in their basement, one of four in the house. This house practically has more storage rooms than my house does rooms, period.

I walk over to Geoff's family's treadmill and I look up at this stone fireplace thing they've got, and my eyes rest on the mantel, where an expensive-looking Chinese vase sits shiny and still. The vase looks so familiar, and when I realize why, it wallops me hard like some sports metaphor involving a stray ball that I won't even attempt.

"I'll be right back," Geoff calls. "Stay there."

Annabeth's ashes sit in a vase just like this, in our sunroom.

It was a gift from Geoff's mom to my mom. Literally it's the same exact vase, with the same exact "vaguely Oriental" pattern but in a different color. Probably bought on the same day at the same store.

Geoff's mom said she knew Annabeth's favorite color was orange—an odd color for an odd girl—and that she wanted us to have it in case we decided to keep Annabeth's ashes on display.

She'd brought it to the memorial, I was told. I was not at the memorial.

I'd promised my mom I'd say some remarks that day, but, like everything in my life, I put it off until the very last moment. Another promise that became another lie. And so instead of ad-libbing and making a blubbering fool of myself in front of all the first-tiers at school, I was on the floor of my bathroom, wearing earplugs, with my forehead pressed against the coolness of my toilet.

"Okay," Geoff says, entering the room again just as the rage bubbles up in me like when you add Mentos to Coke and it explodes like a geyser.

It comes to me, that is, why I am the kind of mad known as sad.

There is so much about Annabeth's life that will never be: She will never share an Oscar with me. She will never have her kids call me Uncle Win. She will never have kids.

And I was kind of getting used to that concept.

But now, this, *too*: This idea that there are things about Annabeth that actually *happened* that I'll never know? That she and Geoff were sneaking around behind my back merely points out the grimmest truth of all: That there are hours and days and months from her life, an autobiography she'll never get to share with me. She didn't keep a diary that I know of. She called our films her diary, but I think she did it just to humor me.

"Um . . . Quinn?"

Something about Annabeth having this secret with my best and only friend underlines how now she's been relegated to sitting there in an urn in the sunroom, forever not able to answer my questions.

"Why were you so snippy with me at the coffee shop?" I say to Geoff. I can't look at him. I am typing 6-6-6 into the treadmill, just to have the distraction of a beep.

"It was our anniversary," he says.

"What?"

"When you came to Loco Mocha yesterday, it was my anniversary with Annabeth. It would have been a year. I was really upset that I couldn't share that, like, heaviness with you."

"Wait, you were seriously officially *dating*?"

"Yeah, when we could sneak in time behind your back, which actually wasn't that hard. You never notice anything if it's not about you."

I step off the treadmill and back Geoff into the sofa.

"We were in *love* with each other," he says.

I am holding so many feelings inside that my body is the second Civil War. "Just stop *talking*. For a *second. Okay?*"

Geoff's eyes spill over. "I lost her too, you know. You don't own the trademark on mourning your sister."

I reach to touch him, and a breeze sweeps through the

basement—*Annabeth's ghost?* I'm thinking—but it's not. It's the vortex created by the door at the top of his stairs opening, and I hear his mom's voice: "Geoff, everything okay down there?" and God love the kid, he goes, "No," and he is crying and not trying to hide the brokenness from his mom, "it's not," and she scurries down the stairs and comes to the French doors leading to the basement. She is in a silk robe. Her hair is up and although she is thin, my mom is prettier.

"Quinn," she says.

I turn away and put the metal apple down, afraid I may launch it at any moment.

"I told him," Geoff says, "but I don't think he believes me."

"No, I do," I'm saying, but then he says: "Tell him, Mom. Tell him how in love with Annabeth I was."

I can't handle this. Hell, I could barely handle that Annabeth never got to have a boyfriend, but now this: that Annabeth was in *love* with somebody and then had that taken away from her? It's too tragic.

"I just can't. This is so not like you guys to keep something from me."

"This is exactly why we didn't tell you," Geoff says. He gets up from the sofa.

"Boys," his mom says. She used to say the same thing when we were in sixth grade and we would tell sex jokes in the backseat of yet another brand-new Toyota. Sex jokes that we thought his mom wouldn't "get."

"The whole world isn't yours to decide, Quinn," Geoff says, and when he's jabbing his finger into my chest, that's when I notice the strange manila envelope in his other hand, the thing he retrieved from storage.

"*Boys*," his mom says again, "come on. Let's cool down and meet up again tomorrow."

"Mom, get out of here. It's fine," Geoff says, but it isn't, and he's scaring me. Geoff is the optimist. Geoff isn't the one to jab or get violent. His parents had a no-hitting rule.

Mine didn't.

"Were you ever going to tell me?" I say. From overhead, we must look like a pretty good setup to a pretty dynamic scene: the aging architect in the robe, the weird kid in the fake glasses, the best friend with the mystery envelope. It's not a bad scenario, if only I knew the ending.

"No," Geoff says, "because when Annabeth went to college, we were going to break up."

He falls back into the couch and puts his head in his hands and plainly sobs, and as he sobs, goobs of snot and spittle fall from his face like Fallingwater, the field trip all Pennsylvanian children are required to take at least twice, and when the goobs fall forth, they land on the manila envelope by his feet, with a return address from Los Angeles, with the word CONGRATS printed across the front, and with my name, QUINN ROBERTS, written above Geoff's address—the word URGENT stamped in red ink.

"What the hell is that?" I say.

"Language," Geoff's mom says, and the three of us somehow laugh. As if *hell* is the worst thing I've ever said, or the worst concept I've ever imagined. Hell is your big sister losing her virginity to your best friend and neither one of them being confident enough to share that news with you because you are, in fact, the monster of this picture. Godzilla got to be the title role, but, my God, he was still the monster. Still the antagonist. Still the wickedest. That is me. The creature who destroys villages and has to be tiptoed around.

"Open it," Geoff says. "Happy fucking birthday." He looks up like a little boy might. His mom wants to say "Language," again, but she doesn't.

I reach for the envelope. My hands are shuddering. I am hungry or perhaps horny. I have never wondered what Geoff would look like naked, but now, suddenly, knowing that he has had sex makes me feel as if I'm meeting a celebrity.

"Why?" I ask, when I open the envelope and my eyes scan the letter. I don't even know what I mean, but that is the word. "Why?" I say again as I read the one-pager from the Los Angeles Society of Young Filmmakers.

"Dear Mr. Roberts," it says—as if I'm my dad. *"Thank you for applying to the Los Angeles Society of Young Filmmakers summer lab!"*

"I didn't apply to this lab," I say. "I never finished the applic—what the hell is this?"

"Keep reading," Geoff says. His cheeks are stained a translucent white, either zit medication running from the tears or maybe just sunblock. No. Definitely sunblock. Geoff doesn't need zit medication.

"I'm going to get you boys a snack," Geoff's mom says, taking off. Leave it to a mom to solve any problem with a snack, and yet: They are always right about this.

We are writing to inform you that your screenplay
Double Digits has been chosen as a finalist for the

X screenwriters

__ directors

division of the LASYF for this August.

As you no doubt know, only 5 screenwriters and
5 directors are chosen each summer, out of submissions that number in the thousands. You were
number one on the wait list, and due to a technical
eligibility requirement not being met by a previous finalist, we are delighted to accept you into
our upcoming lab.

Please note the URGENT nature of the following:

-If you wish to attend, we will need to hear from you by August 1 for an August 18 start in Los Angeles.

-We are unable to supply housing or airfare.

-Most vitally, we cannot accept incomplete screenplays; you must supply the final pages to us by August 1, the same date as the official opt-out, or we will have to ask you to reapply again in the future.

Please reply at your earliest convenience, and congratulations again on the thrilling first draft of *Double Digits*. We look forward to pairing you with a student director in Los Angeles.

Sincerely,

Gloria Katz

Chair, the LASYF

Geoff's mom reappears in the doorway with a tray. This breaks my heart. My poor mom would never think to serve something on a tray. The snack would never even make it out of the kitchen.

"I don't understand anything anymore," I say to Geoff. "Annabeth and I didn't apply to this. I don't understand this."

Nobody has read that script except my sister, who found it "limited" and said it wasn't my best work of all time and was going to be "impossible to direct." That it could use professional guidance. That she wished Ricky Devlin were still around to mentor me—"*or we could just apply to* this," she wrote, when she forwarded me the link to the lab in LA. I printed out the application that night, feeling smug for such an accomplishment, as if the damn thing would just fill out its own pages.

"Annabeth and I applied for you," Geoff says.

(beat) (beat) (beat)

"What the fuck are you talking about?" I say. But I am so quiet that I scare myself. Geoff's mom's lips mouth the word "Language" but they don't say it.

"If your script wins at the end of the lab," Geoff says, taking a baked pita chip from the tray, "*Double Digits* will get screened on some festival circuit."

I bounce a little, as if prepping to spring away to the moon, or even better, directly into the sun. "What are you—that is the, like, working title. That isn't even—nobody was supposed to see that, except her. I specifically *didn't* apply because the screenplay wasn't *ready*."

"I know," Geoff says, droll. "But Annabeth and I were tired of seeing you being so precious about every last little thing."

"*Sweetie,*" his mom says, and he snaps at her: "Give us some space, Mom."

Never mind. He doesn't snap. I forgot that in some families, the men are able to ask for what they want without violence edging their voices like burnt paper.

"I'll be right upstairs," his mom says. She's forever working on her architecture plans, forever constructing buildings to behave just the way she wants them to. I get this completely.

"It's a huge opportunity, dude," Geoff says, as if he's Mrs. friggin' Kelly in the cinder-block counselor's room.

"Then why are you *crying*?" I say, and he really is, his face running like Fallingwater again, an unlimited brook of tears.

"Thousands of applicants, screenwriters *and* filmmakers, and you got in."

"We were on the *wait* list," I say, folding the paper in half.

"You got in."

"Then why," I say, again, "are you crying?"

"We sent in the first three-quarters of your screenplay, which wasn't even allowed—it had to be a complete script"—(yes, I know; *that's why I didn't apply*)—"but you got in because you're that fucking good. . . ."

I unfold the page and look at it again:

We are writing to inform you your screenplay
Double Digits has been chosen as a finalist for the

X screenwriters
__ directors

"But the thing is," he goes, "Annabeth didn't want . . . um."

But the way he says "um" makes me know this is not just an *um*. There's always an *and* with Geoff.

"*What?*" I say. "She didn't want *what?*"

"Annabeth didn't want to check off the director's box," Geoff says, a thin film of saliva breaking across his mouth, like the giant bubbles we used to play with back in the summers, when everything was possible. "It would have been the easiest thing to do—to send in her reel and see if she'd get in too—but she was cool just letting this be your thing, Quinny."

"*No.* That doesn't even sound like h—"

"She always said your dialogue was what made the movies pop," Geoff says—and strangely, right at the climax of the scene, right when John Williams would bring in the saddest, lowest horns, to make you cry, Geoff doesn't keep crying. The tears stop and he offers a wounded smile, like a truce. "And she was obviously right."

I look at his mom's vase. "So, wait—now you actually expect me to go to, like, Los *Angeles* and get paired with some anonymous person who isn't your dead girlfriend? *This* is how you want me to celebrate my birthday?"

Never mind. He's crying again. Geoff's Adam's apple jumps up and down like the trampoline in our neighbor's yard. He can't speak. "Mhmm?" he finally manages to hum.

I am all out of dialogue. I walk very slowly to the tray of food, and I pick up the whole thing and almost throw it against his perfect wallpapered wall—it would make for such a strong, complicated goodbye.

But I am not going to be that guy.

So all I do is set down the tray and tear the paper in half, and crumple it up, and throw it at Geoff.

"She didn't want this dream, Quinn," he says, finally, when I'm putting the bowling shoes on again, with my back to him. "But you do. Or did."

I push through the French doors. I don't even stop when Geoff's mom tries to hug me by their kitchen island. And by the time I'm ten minutes out of the good part of town, I get this somewhat fucked-up idea for how to turn my birthday around. How to even the score with my best friend, with the universe. How to play catch-up with my sister.

"**What was that you said,**" I text Amir, just as I'm getting to my neighborhood, "**about getting me laid tonight?**"

CHAPTER THIRTY

One shower later, I'm sitting outside on our crumbly front steps, picking at a scab on my knee that I didn't even know had been scabbed. What I'm *not* doing is I'm not walking up the street and waiting for Amir to pick me up there. I'm just letting him show up outside our house in plain sight. I suppose I'm coming out in twelve easy steps.

It is 10:59 p.m. when I see his dirty Saturn peep up from the top of our hill.

"No fair," he goes, when he pulls up and I step in. "You got to clean up after my party."

"I have some CK One upstairs. You want me to run in and get you some?"

But he doesn't, and I don't, and what we do is we drive back to the bowling lanes, so I can get my old Vans and give them back their bowling shoes and start to reset the world back to its old ways.

"Hey," he says, "buckle up," just as we're speeding past the high school.

Something about watching Amir drive stick shift is maybe the hottest thing ever, did I already say that? He is just so *forceful* with it.

"So," he says. Now we're sitting in the parking lot of the bowling alley. It's late, officially very much not my birthday. Officially next year. "I was kind of surprised to hear from you tonight. I mean, after."

"Yeah, well," I say, "I felt kind of embarrassed about running away from your boat and I wanted to apologize." Lie. I want to get laid.

"I'm really sorry that Carly broke the news about Geoff and your sister," Amir goes. "It was seriously uncool of her. For the record, *I* had no ide—"

"Carly lives on gossip. It's just Carly being Carly."

A bird spins itself in nervous circles right above Amir's windshield. It must be lost. It's too late for a bird to be away from its tree.

"Should we go back to my place?" He's already turning the car back on, and my heart starts to go faster than I want it to. I don't like not being in control, and it feels as if a riverboat is in my chest, churning against my stomach.

"Sure thing," I say, practically like I mean it.

· · ·

It takes a three-floor trek upstairs to an apartment covered in boxes for it to actually hit me that Amir really is going. He is not out of breath, but I am.

"Okay, hang out on the couch," he goes, "and flip the AC on, for the love of God. I'm hopping in the shower." I look up to see this perfect shirtless boy, his boxers puffed out the top of his shorts like a muffin, a small scar on his stomach existing only to show, in stark contrast, how flawless the rest of him is.

When he's gone, I take my own shirt off and hold my phone out far and look at myself in the reverse camera and oh my God I hope he likes truly skinny guys.

The shower *cheep-cheeps* off. I put my shirt back on. I debate about running for it.

"Should I put some music on?" he calls out, and I go, "Mhmm, okay," and he returns in mesh shorts and a tank top and this Texas ball cap that makes me want to eat him, it is so cute.

Mesh shorts on guys are my weakness, by the way. Mesh shorts are the "coming attractions" of the hot-boy clothing world.

He sits on the sofa and hands me his laptop, and goes: "You have to pick what you want to listen to," so I take Amir's laptop and though I guess I'm supposed to be picking out make-out music, instead I multitask and say: "*Morning Pages*, what's *Morning Pages*?"—looking at the only file on his desktop.

Amir reaches across and takes the laptop out of my lap faster than you can say calm down.

"Nothing," he goes.

"Well, it's *something*," I go, and he rolls his eyes and goes: "It's kind of like a journal. I wake up every day and write three tangential pages back to back."

I smile my best sly smile. I've practiced it in the mirror for years. "Okay," I say. "And yet you're going to school for *business* and not writing?"

He lies back on the couch and digs his feet underneath my butt, and it is very sweet.

"You should read me some of these *Morning Pages*," I say, and he laughs and goes, "Oh, I so should *not* do that."

I reach my arm back to lay it across the couch, and my elbow grazes a picture frame, which tips over and lands with a solid *clack*. I worry that maybe I've cracked the glass, but when I set it up again, it is not broken. It is a perfect unharmed photo of two guys—Amir, next to somebody Dad-age.

"Who's that?" I say, and the way Amir goes, "Oh, that's Evan," I know it's over.

"How long were you together?" I'm not doing the flirty-mouth thing anymore.

"Well, *that's* presumptuous," Amir says. He wiggles his toes and it tickles my butt. I squirm, but I don't laugh. This night has no clear ending; it's all middle.

I pick up the photo and launch an investigation. Clue number one: Evan is holding Amir's waist.

"A year and a half," Amir says finally, and then: "Until he fucking *cheated* on me with one of his students."

The AC clicks off. "Where is he now?"

"Back in Texas," he says, and I go, "Back in Texas," because I like when dialogue echoes, except not this time.

I am in a brain fog when Amir opens his laptop back up and turns on some music that sounds familiar—something rousing and orchestral and more cinematic, somehow, than straightforward trumpets usually are—and I know it I know it I know it, and finally I go: "Wait, don't tell me," and Amir smiles and goes, "I wasn't going to."

He gets up close to my face and kisses my forehead. *Chug-chug-chug,* the riverboat is back in my chest.

"Read something to me," I say, because suddenly I'm back to being unsure if I'm ready to have sex.

"What do you mean?" he goes.

"Read me some of your work. Out loud."

"Only if you do," he goes, and he plops back onto the sofa.

"No way," I go. "My stuff is junk and I don't have any of it on me."

"You don't back it up in the cloud?"

"Well, yeah, but—"

He puts his laptop on my lap. Spotify is minimized. The trumpets continue to blat and cry.

"I'll read you the first page of my terrible novel if you read me the first page of your terrible screenplay."

"No," I go, "but I'll pull up some Vimeos of my old films with Annabeth and leave the room for fifteen minutes and you can watch whatever you want. Films are meant to be seen, not read."

"Thanks, Mom," he goes, and *that* is getting old faster than hot milk.

He takes the laptop back from me. "I've already watched all your films," he goes, just like that, and I go, "Wait, wh—," and he goes, "After that Celebrity game-night thing, I was all, 'Who is that guy?' and Carly was all, 'You have to see his movies.'"

I stare at a crack across the blank wall of his apartment and expect it to open up and swallow me into a portal. Those weren't my movies. Those were *our* movies.

Change the scene. Switch the topic. Take control of the narrative.

It comes to me: "Elmer Bernstein," I say.

It's just, Elmer Bernstein has a very distinctive cinematic underscoring style, and his music is drowning out this conversation on Amir's couch. (Thank you, Mr. Bernstein.)

"Correct." Amir smiles. "You *are* good." He double-clicks and then double-clicks again, and then: "I've never done this."

"Um . . ."

"Read my work out loud."

Oh! This is kind of fun. I can be the loyal guy Evan never was, and this will convince Amir to stay here. I will move in with him next year. I will work at Carnegie Library and watch DVDs all day. We will have brown babies because we will use his DNA.

"I'm waiting," I say, pointing to the computer.

He turns the volume down on Elmer Bernstein and clears his throat and he puts his feet on my lap, and they smell just faintly faintly faintly like boy feet and something about that is very wonderful. Maybe I do want to have sex. It seems like I only want to have sex when I'm not thinking about it, and I only don't want to have sex when I am.

"Okay, so . . . ," Amir goes, and I go, "Stalling!" and he goes, "No, wait," and his eyes are scanning page one—just like mine always did right before I would read my first drafts for Annabeth—and he goes, "I'm not sure about this," and I go, "Come on, isn't this the novel that got you into this prestigious program?" and when I say it out loud, I'm thinking about what it would be like for me to go to LA and be paired with some anonymous new director, and that's just one big fat no, right there.

The Wachowskis. The Ephron sisters. The Nolans. Q & A.

I've been alive for seventeen *years*; how is some brand-new director going to be able to decode all the nuances and jokes and not-jokes in my work?

"So . . . okay," Amir says. He takes his feet off my lap and turns around so that his back is totally facing me.

"What are you doing?" I go.

"I just said I couldn't read it out loud if I was facing you."

"Oh, yeah, of course," I lie. The AC clicks itself off again. The Elmer Bernstein continues on a loop from Amir's computer, the same song on repeat. Trumpet, trumpet, trumpet.

"Chapter one," Amir says, "page one *only*." He faux-coughs twice and goes, "I can't believe I'm doing this," and I go, "That's a compelling first line," and he goes, *"Quinn,"* and I shut up.

"Marleek Tabasian," Amir says, his voice small, *"awakened earlier than she had in months because the heat was eating her from the inside out. This was unusual even for Lindandia, which was carved into the earth two thousand years after the Great Lindandian fall. . . ."*

I hold my breath. His work is possibly . . . terrible, yes, that's the word, terrible, and so I put my feet against his back so that he feels he has my support. It's amazing how much you can fake, physically. Just ask Marlon Brando, who literally *couldn't really speak* and was the best actor of all time.

"Marleek's spirit mother, Tasia Tabasian," he continues, getting louder and unfortunately more confident, *"was already in the study, looking over the day's agenda. She startled at the sight of her spirit daughter, unclothed and floating."*

Oh, dear. I pull my feet away. Even my feet can't fake it in the face of this hokum.

But then something changes.

Amir's voice gets stronger and softer, at the same time, and I'm able to hear that his writing is stilted but ambitious, which describes perhaps the opposite of my whole life—articulate but lazy. You can tell he has created a world that he believes in, or wants his readers to, and by the end of page one, I am able to appreciate the fact that he is attempting something. That he is, at least, not hibernating.

"Okay, blah," he goes, swinging back around, "end of page one. That's it. Ahh, I want to kill myself."

"Don't say that, it was wonderful."

"No, it wasn't," he says, but he's not exactly looking away from me. "Your turn," he goes, setting the laptop on my legs. "Page one of your screenplay."

"No," I say, somehow working a lighthearted laugh into the proceedings. "Seriously, no way."

"Then you're not getting laid," he goes, as if he's punishing me, which he is.

We have a staring contest and dammit he wins. Trumpets, trumpets, trumpets.

I open up a new tab and type in my cloud password and scroll through all my screenplays—and for a moment I truly do debate reading from *Double Digits*. When I open up the first page, I can't help at least smile at how very me it is.

But then I read this jokey character description that always made her giggle—the first scene of the screenplay started with me describing the title character as *"a fierce young warrior, and I don't mean 'gay' fierce"*—and right here on this sofa, I can hear Annabeth cackling at that turn of phrase, and just, *no*: "I'm not doing this, Amir," I say, letting my eyes rest on the phrase *fierce young warrior*. "Only my sister got to hear my bad line readings."

I look over the laptop screen and Amir is pulling off his mesh shorts. "Are you *sure* you won't even read one *page*?" he says. He is in purple briefs. He is beautiful. He is both a badger and a butterfly.

Trumpets, trumpets, trumpets. (beat) (beat) (beat)

I lick my lips, not to flirt but to prepare. I close my eyes and count backward from ten, telling myself I'll know by the time I hit "one." But I know by the time I hit "nine."

"I'm just not ready," I say. I look up. The smallest saliva bubble has formed on Amir's lips, and I don't care. His imperfections are his perfections. Ten beautiful fingers creep up over his computer, and when the screen clamps silently shut, the trumpets continue to play for one more moment, as if Elmer Bernstein's little orchestra of tiny people is trapped inside the laptop. Amir is shirtless, his tank top has disappeared, his hat is on the floor, his hair is matted down. He is smiling, but it is a sex smile, not any other kind. I know this instantly because nobody has ever smiled at me like this, and so it must be that.

"Well, I still think you're a genius," he says, and I go, "Careful. If you keep saying that, I might believe you."

He takes the laptop and puts it on his coffee table. It is in this moment that I understand that Amir is not a genius, himself—at least not at storytelling. I replay the first page of his novel in my mind, and I decide that a future in "business" might be good for Amir. He is not a genius, and rereading the first page of *Double Digits* to myself makes me wonder if in some small way I've been comparing myself to the great film-makers too early in my career. Amir is older than me, but I am a more talented writer; this I know.

If he feels confident enough to even *try* writing "the great Iranian-American novel," maybe I shouldn't give up so easily on attempting my own personal, like, great American whatever.

"How much of your novel did you have to submit before getting accepted into the San Francisco thing?" I ask. I can feel my lip twitching.

He karate-chops a cushion. "None of it."

"What?"

"Evan's brother runs the program, and I got in as a favor, and I never submitted any writing. So. Can we not talk about this right now?"

I nod.

He pulls me up and grabs the bottom ridge of my shirt, and I feel an air-conditioned coolness on my stomach and I jut my elbows down and push his hands away.

"What?" he goes. "Do you not want to do this?"

His breath smells like breath, not unpleasant but definitely human.

"I'm really self-conscious about my body," I say, but he takes my hands and leads me out of the bright-ass living room.

He does not have an AC in his bedroom, but then he barely has a bed: A mattress sits on the floor, with a paisley sheet thrown across, with boxes surrounding it, with boy clothes piled on a chair. "I packed everything up," he goes, and then: "Is it too hot in here?" and I say: "No, not at all," because I am freezing, as if I have a fever. My riverboat chest has hit an iceberg after all.

He pulls my shirt off over my head, and I hunch my shoulders in and wish I had my bangs back, to brush down into my face. And when he takes off my glasses and then his own, and tries mine on without asking, and goes, "Wait, are these fakes?" I want to yell that everything is, Amir. Everything is fake.

He puts his glasses back on and places mine on the mattress. "You shouldn't be self-conscious of your body," he says. "Like, at all." His fingers are tracing the bony tracks of my chest.

I am completely hard only as a reaction to physical touch but not out of anticipation or even horniness. I am kind of petrified I will do everything wrong. Evan the Ex is so much older than I am. They must have had tricks, techniques, and inside jokes. Even in the bedroom. God knows I've seen enough porn to at least have a basic sense of the etiquette and approach to this stuff, but then again, I've watched a lot of YouTubes of Olympic divers, too—those bathing suits, *those bathing suits*—and I'm no closer to flipping off a forty-foot platform than I am to winning an Oscar.

"Hey," Amir says, and he kisses my nose, "distracted boy."

I kiss him back, this time with a medium amount of tongue, and we fall onto his mattress, and a streetlight spills into the room through blinds that make Amir look like a beautiful striped zebra—as exotic and endangered as every boy has ever felt to me.

"I'm so sad," I say, to buy some time, but also to try out what that sounds like, and he goes: "Aww, about me leaving?" And I say: "No—sorry. I mean, yes. But I am so sad that my sister and my best friend didn't trust me enough to tell me they were, like, a thing."

In all these months I have never once said I am sad, not out loud, maybe because it's so obvious that it seems a little on the nose to verbalize. I hate being ordinary.

But now that I've said it, it pulses like a blue bug zapper. I am sad. Pulse. Pulse. Pulse. *Zap.*

"Do you want to, like, talk about it?"

"Nah," I say. "I just wanted to name it."

"Okay." Pause. He places his hand on my stomach, dangerously close to Boner Zone. "I still think you're adorable."

"More making out," I say, sniffing, "less talking."

And that's the cue to have epic sex—it just is—but then we don't have even normal sex. Not at all. We *talk.* We talk about what it's like to be embarrassed about being somebody's kid, and we talk about how strangely coordinated we both were at Little League, and we talk about what we think happens to somebody's, like, soul, when they die ("Absolutely nothing," we both conclude).

And we talk about how weird it is to burn a loved one into

a fine powder and then put her into a fifteen-dollar orange jar, and what it's like to be young but feel old, and why we both want to tell stories, and why Pittsburgh is wonderful. We talk about Evan and we talk about my dad. We talk about how both our balloons got caught on the guardrail of the roof on the night we met, and we talk about how neither of us really believes in signs or coincidences, except: The way we say it, I think we're both still holding out hope that perhaps, perhaps.

Fully an hour later we're talking about how Amir is semi-allergic to lactose and about how I am fully allergic to optimism, and though it's my best piece of dialogue all week, neither of us even smiles at it.

At some point I nod off, and at another point I wake up and he is looking right at me, and I say, "I don't think this is going to happen tonight," and he goes, "I sort of figured that out an hour ago," and then it's his turn to drift off, as though I am keeping guard of the campsite so he can get a few winks in before the bears return, before life happens again.

My mouth is dry because it has said too many words. I put my shirt back on. I walk out to the living room, and I'm not *exactly* proud of this, but I find Amir's laptop and I open the screen, and when there is no password to have to guess at (I would have tried "Evan123" and then "evan4ever"), I hit mute on Elmer Bernstein's violins and I open Amir's *Morning Pages* daily diary and I scroll and I scroll and I see something shocking and true involving me.

I see that in the days since Amir met me, he hasn't written about Quinn Roberts. Not even once. He has written only about Evan, but maybe all my years of faking an uptight-detective voice for my mom have paid off, because I feel I have solved a true mystery: Amir has always been the younger guy. Finally, with me, he can be older. He can even the score. He is not *my* prop, tonight—I am his. That is all this is or was, not that Amir and I were ever enough of a thing to even be a was.

"Um," he says. He is somehow standing before me in those purple briefs. I fumble to x out of his *Morning Pages* Word document, and I say, "Sorry, just checking my e-mail," and he squinches his face up at me again and goes, "Uh, okay," and bends down to pick up his shorts and his tank top and his hat. And he hands me back my fake glasses.

Other than reminding me to buckle up, Amir wordlessly drives me back home, but before I get out he turns down NPR and goes: "The great escape," and I say, "I'm sorry?" and he says: "The Bernstein score. At my place. That's what I was playing for you."

"Oh, right," I say, of course, "*The Great Escape*. Good movie."

"Yeah," he says.

The porch lights aren't flashing tonight, and so I give myself the luxury of one more minute, and go, "Trivia."

He laughs. "Okay, Trivia. Can't wait."

"First question: Am I a joke to you?"

"Uh. What?"

"Sorry. Just: Have I just been, like, some anonymous kid to potentially fuck around with just so you could get even with Evan?"

Amir takes my hand and puts it on his lap. He is completely hard. "Does this," he says, "feel anonymous to you?"

And because I am not expecting it at all—because I had completely given up on the idea of losing my virginity tonight—this time, I don't write a sex scene. I just have one.

He unbuckles himself and reclines his seat, and I mount him as if he is, in fact, that escaped and exotic zebra: I'm fumbling for his zipper, exploring the scar on his stomach, kissing him so hard our teeth clatter, or maybe that's just because I'm freezing cold, again, and absolutely shaking.

"Do you want me to turn the heat on?" he whispers, like my mom might be hiding in the backseat, and I say, "No, I want you to drive us down the street, with your headlights off."

I climb off him back into my seat, cross my legs like a lady at a beauty salon, and touch my swollen lips, which I discover are smiling, which are burning like something alive and rubbed raw by a real live man's face.

Two minutes later we are parked beneath an ancient weeping willow on an abandoned lot, naked in the backseat of Amir's Saturn, our limbs intertwined like mixed-race pretzels, the moon so overcast that for one brief, funny moment, I think that if a cop approached the car with a flashlight, we might look like siblings with the same exact color skin and height, wrestling.

When Amir pulls off one of his socks to clean us up, we laugh—"We kept our socks on," we say at the same time, and then, "Jinx"—and he goes, "That doesn't always happen with two people, just FYI: the, uh, 'finishing at the same time' thing."

I go, "Cool," pull my lucky boxers back up, and scramble into the front seat, where I look up to see not a lost bird outside Amir's windshield, but instead a black ribbon, tied to the willow tree we'd nearly driven into. And I am not freezing anymore.

We kiss one more time, and the way he goes, "Obviously we're keeping in touch," after the little drive back up to my house, and the way I go, "Obviously, duh," back, makes me understand that I am somehow not at all sad that I am never going to see him again.

CHAPTER THIRTY-ONE

Mom must be in her bedroom, because the sunroom light is off. The house feels burglarized, somehow, unsettlingly altered by the mere act of cleaning it.

I wash Amir off my hands. There's a silver dollar on the kitchen counter with a Post-it note on it: *"More loot for my birthday boy,"* it says. Our house is a strange nighttime pirate cove. Mom's parents left her nothing when they died, and yet now it is as if our old house is bleeding treasure at every turn.

I'm walking up the stairs, and each of its steps is behaving tonight. In the humidity they have stopped crying out and have decided to cooperate. Though I've gotten used to coasting right by Annabeth's room, I've still never gone back in, but tonight I look at the door and I feel it pulsing. Pulse. Pulse. Pulse. *Zap.*

I feel it asking me to enter, as if to say: *We are the same now. We are no longer virgins.* And so I go in.

I open the door and this is it: Her room is the final show-down. I know this instantly. It must be. Her room is the secret monster I haven't met yet. This is the level I must pass.

I am Ripley and her room is the Alien Queen (*Aliens*).

I am Rocky Balboa and her room is Apollo Creed (*Rocky*).

I am Dirty Harry and her room is the Scorpio Killer (*Dirty Harry*).

Ever notice that in the old days, they just named the villain or the protagonist right in the title? The title of my movie might just be *Quinn*, the rare film in which the audience isn't sure at the end if the lead was the good guy or the bad guy.

I walk to her bed and I fall to my knees in a silent crash. The Elmer Bernstein trumpets start back up in my head, a loop that drives me nuts. I bury my face in Annabeth's scratchy polyester comforter, and I slide down and droop over and melt into the floor, and I am suddenly looking at a metal box. I don't know this metal box.

I pull it out from beneath her bed and I lift the box's cover. There is an orange-and-gray-striped diary inside, and I hold it tight and feel that I cannot be here: I cannot do this in this room. I stand up and power walk across the hall to my room, which is precisely three hundred times as hot as Annabeth's.

We got our twin beds on the exact same day—they were actually a matching set—and so I re-create the scene back in my sister's room and I lie on the floor next to my bed and I open her diary to a random page.

"Dream Schools," it says at the top. She has made a graph, which is so her. Under *"Dream Schools"* she has listed seven of them. She has written *"Dream Majors"* next to *"Dream Schools"* and created an orderly column, and her dream majors were Communications *"and/or"* Spanish.

My sister's dream major was Spanish? She was dating Geoff and her dream major was Spanish? And what else that I'll never know.

Here is what she never said in her diary, because I'm flipping through it now so fast, the pages might start smoking and I wouldn't blink: She never said her dream major was Cinema Studies. She never said her dream major was Filmmaking. She never said she wanted that. This genuinely surprises me.

I page through in order to find something happier. And I do. I see the phrase *"Win is driving me F'ING NUTS today,"* from like two years ago, and now, *now,* now I burst into tears, happy tears, happy to read a new truth from my sister. I never thought I'd get to hear a new truth from her.

And then more: *"G. says Win looked at him funny today and that he hopes when Win comes out to him it's not as a confession that he's in love with him,"* and then, on another page, *"G. didn't want to have sex (he said he doesn't want it to throw off the dynamic between us??) but I pushed and he relented and we had completely awkward and actually PAINFUL but also kind of funny sex and I WANT MORE MWAHAHA,"* and I look at the wall like I'm in a sitcom and can't believe the straitlaced sister character just said that. I wait for the laugh track, but I'm still hearing only trumpets. I flip to another page and it says: *"G. is VAGUELY desperate for Win to apply to this film contest so he can be out of our hair this summer and we won't have to sneak arouuuunnnnnd anymore,"* and I don't let myself register any of that, none of it, and instead I turn five pages ahead to find: *"G. and I talked about breaking up when I go away to school, but it is hard to imagine meeting somebody who is as good of a fit for me."*

This is the only revelation that makes me mad, because you know who was the perfect fit for her? I was.

People used to think we were twins, even.

I close the box and also my eyes, and I slide the box beneath my twin-size bed and it hits something with the very same *clack* that the photo of Amir and Evan made, when my elbow went on a secret mission tonight to knock over their photo.

I push Annabeth's box out of the way and squint, but it's endlessly dark beneath my bed, and so I reach my arm beneath it and feel around, and when I grab the thing that made the *clack*, it's as if I've found the sword or the poison, one or the other: the weapon or elixir that is meant to send the hero of every screenplay home reborn. Because there's no place, of course, like home.

Except, I'm already home.

The trumpets in my head are now manic, *blatting* all over the place, Elmer Bernstein's arms sagging in exhaustion after conducting this insane orchestra not of tiny people but of huge ones, of demons, of Ricky and my father and most of all of me.

It's my old cell phone. I have found it.

I pull it out from beneath my bed, and I shake the dust bunnies from my arm, and when I stand, the floors give and hum, and maybe I should have shut my door, because I'm making enough ruckus in here that when I sit on my bed and look at this black box recorder that holds Annabeth's final message to me like a dead girl's fist, Mom is just above the movie frame, in the doorway, looking at me like I am no longer a virgin.

And just like that, the trumpets stop.

CHAPTER THIRTY-TWO

"Hey"

"hey, morning, whats up. at work"

"You have a minute to talk"

"no quinn I'm >>>>AT WORK<<<< SOME PEOPLE WORK"

"Hahahah"

"haha"

"Hahahhahahahaha"

"hahahah"

I'm standing in my backyard, right over the makeshift pit Dad and I used to make illegal fires in. It's basically overgrown now, so lush you have to dull out your eyes to see the charred-out, mossy cement blocks from before. Our backyard could really be something. We've got a lot of space. If I ever actually sell a screenplay, you can screw my Hollywood

Hills backyard. I'm buying a pool for Mom here; I just am.

"I found my old phone last night," I send.

"um . . . ok?"

"I plugged it in haven't turned it on yet i want to say something else tho"

"calling you in 5"

And so he does, exactly five minutes later. Geoff is the picture of punctuality now that he has a job. We are getting older so fast these days. It's fucking *eerie*.

"What's up?" he goes.

"First off, I'm sorry that I freaked out on you last night and almost threw your mom's metal fruit at the wall in the basement."

Sigh. "Yep."

"And that I threw the acceptance letter thing at your face. I have such bad aim, usually."

I'm waiting for him to snort-laugh, but instead I hear a version of a cough happen on the other side of the phone—the same throaty thing he's done since I first saw him cry, when we were five and I yanked the truck out of his hand and he wept so quietly that it was the day I learned that a person can make you feel guiltier by underreacting.

"I should, um," Geoff finally goes, and I say, "Go for it," and I hold my new phone to my ear for one second longer and hear him tell a customer to "just take the drink" and that he was "sorry for being rude."

I've gotta stop forcing people to be rude on my behalf.

Right before I hang up, Geoff comes back and goes, "Win?"

"Yeah?" I guess everybody's calling me Win now.

"Wanna go to the pool with me and Carly this afternoon? I think she wants to apologize to you. You can bring your boyfriend."

I pull a weed out from between two fire-pit cinder blocks. The weed is pricklier than I'd anticipated, and it makes the cardboard cut on my hand scream like it's in a silent movie.

"Uh, no," I say. "I think Amir and I are a past-tense thing now."

"Oh. Dude."

"But, *yes*. I want to go to the pool. So hard."

"Gimme twenty and I'm off work," Geoff goes, and I'm saying, "Hey, if I can't make it rain this summer, at least I'll get wet today," and it's such a cheesy piece of dialogue that I'm glad he's already hung up.

When I'm back in my room a minute later, I slip on my old swim trunks, expecting them to be snug. Isn't every seventeen-year-old boy supposed to outgrow his clothes, like, every two weeks? But I'm so skinny, they practically pool at my feet. So I double-knot them twice, and I unplug my old phone from the wall and throw it in my bookbag. And as I head out, I touch Annabeth's door on the way to the stairs.

CHAPTER THIRTY-THREE

We're right in the middle of an *annoyyyying* conversation about this movie contest in LA when, "Shit," Geoff says. He pulls his Corolla off the parkway without using the turn signal.

"What?"

"I forgot I have to pick up Carly in Mount Lebo," he goes, and that cracks us both up. We almost forgot an entire other human on our way to the country-club pool. I'm glad for the distraction, for the tonal shift, for the introduction of a B-story. But Geoff picks "the talk" right back up.

"Seriously, if you don't do this writing lab thing, you're crazy."

So I jump right back in too. "How would my mom afford a ticket to LA? Where would I stay? Nothing about it makes sen—"

"You could stay with Ricky Devlin," Geoff goes, and I roll my eyes hard enough that I bet he can hear the sockets creaking. "We could find you a cheap flight."

"We have different definitions of 'a cheap flight,'" I say. "In my family a cheap flight is jumping off the roof and landing on a mattress."

Geoff laughs. We used to actually do this together until he broke his ankle in fifth grade.

"And, anyway, whatever." I'm worried he'll offer to pay for the flight, so I talk fast: "This was written to be *our* movie together, not some rando director's in LA."

"You're out of your mind," Geoff goes. "She didn't even apply, Win. She would have been really, really happy for you to get out of her hair and meet a director who really *wanted* to be a director." He's doing the thing I hate where he steers with his knee. "Just *finish* the damn screenplay and get *over* yourself."

"*No*, I would need a bigger sign. She was probably just humoring you."

"Uh, Annabeth *never* humo—"

"Maybe she would have changed her *mind* about me going without her, once I actually got in—and could you *please* use, like, *one* hand to drive? *Just one.*"

In some families, the guys do snap at each other.

"Jeez, Louise."

Ignore. Talk quieter. "I'd need a sign."

Awkward pause, and then Geoff makes the tiniest girl voice and keeps his mouth still and squeaks out, *"Win, I want you to go,"* and I punch his arm and go, "That's not funny," and that's usually where we'd bust out laughing, but we don't.

I reach into his glove compartment for a Jolly Rancher, but they're all gone.

We're driving past the Presbyterian church, and I shouldn't be surprised when we stop at a red light next to the Liberty, but I am, because of what I see.

Green light, and then: "Oh my God, stop," I say, and Geoff goes, "What? Why?" and I go, "Pull over!" and I jump out before he stops.

"Excuse me," I shout like a crazy person, dashing through the cars. I lose a flip-flop in the street, but I keep going, running to this blond woman who is pulling down the "for rent" sign outside the Liberty. "Excuse me, are you Jen?" I say.

She sure looks just like Jennifer "Jen" Richart, whose shiny happy Realtor face is still splattered across the building.

"Rick?" she says weirdly.

"No, no," I say, "I'm not—I'm Win. My name is Win. Anyway—"

"Dude, what are you doing?" Geoff has the Corolla double-parked. He's got the passenger window rolled down and is kind of hollering at me.

"One sec," I say, and whip my head back to Jen. "What's going on here?"

"Somebody put in a bid on this place," she goes, crumpling the "for rent" poster into her stomach. She looks tired but happy.

"Wait, to, like, turn it back into—," but then I stop. I know the ending.

I know the whole story already. My mind is blown open, and instead of brain splatter, what happens is a thousand fire-crackers burst out of my ears.

"Dude, come *on*. Carly's texting me."

"Thank you for not renting this out as a pharmacy or a bank," I say, and "Jen" goes, "Don't thank me. Thank the buyer."

I tear down a big handful of flyers from the ticket window, and then another, and I stuff them in a garbage can on the curb and get into G.'s Corolla.

"Sorry," I say, flopping back into the car seat, "but that was the craziest thing ever. I think Ricky fucking Devlin might be *buying* the fucking Liberty," and Geoff steals my catchphrase and goes, "No way," and I steal Amir's and go, "Way." And as we take off again to pick up Carly, Geoff turns down the song of the summer, and I'm thinking he's gonna nag me to buckle up, but instead he just goes: "Sounds like a sign to me."

"Put it all on account nineteen-eighty," Geoff says to the cashier, before we take our trays to find some shade. OPEN QUESTION: Can somebody be considered a cashier if they never actually deal with cash? Regardless, it's a fundamental universal law that there is nothing better than poolside corn dogs that somebody else's dad is funding.

"You two gross me out eating those things, seriously," Carly goes, and Geoff and I stop chewing and we lock eyes and for two seconds almost make gross animal noises, but somehow we skip that today. Besides, I brought the rest of my ice cream cake to the pool, and it's time for dessert. Today's the six-month anniversary. We never miss a half birthday, though this is more of a half deathday, I suppose.

"Dude," Geoff says. He kicks my knee with a neon flip-flop. "You got half-birthday cake on you."

I pull up my tank top to lick it off. Geoff cackles. "I love a dude who fights for his chocolate," he goes, and even Carly lightens up a little and goes, "Chocolate is literally everything," and I look right at her for the first time today.

Just when I think she's going to apologize for all the drama on Amir's boat last night—for spilled secrets that should never have been secrets to begin with; for being kind of mean; for stirring the pot and stirring my life, too—she doesn't. She goes, "Handstand contest?" instead, and I bust into giggles and go, "Duh," and she and I dump our trays and throw away the last piece of cake, and leave Geoff behind—because he can't go upside down in the water (makes him puke, always has, oddest thing).

Not even two seconds later I'm careening into the pool, chocolaty tank top and all, sunglasses and all, hat and all, one flip-flop only, and I'm upside down pressing my hands into the bumpy bottom and feeling my skin pucker up cold and feeling like this is the first time in six months I haven't felt upside down but rather exactly right.

We pop to the surface maybe thirty seconds later. We

haven't done this in years. I can't believe my stamina, though I also think she let me win.

"You let me win," I go, but Carly is shaking her head.

"You were down there for like two minutes. Seriously. It was freaking me out."

Geoff is by the side of the pool, his hands on his hips. From this angle I see that he is going to turn out genuinely cute someday. That sometimes I should let people just make up their own character descriptions.

"I've been holding my breath for six months, I guess," I say, and even though it's a little jokey—all of my dialogue is, so sue me; I'd seriously like to hear *your* first-draft jokes—we all smile at one another. I think at the same moment we all picture how bad Annabeth was at handstands, how she used to come right back up coughing, right away. How she always lost.

And just when that's the saddest little memory—because all the saddest memories are the small ones that creep up on you quiet and scary as a summer bug—Geoff does a cannonball right beside Carly, and soaks her, and we all laugh and shriek.

The lifeguard tells us to knock it "the heck" off, but it's a good moment, which is all you can count on or hope for, I think. Tiny little good moments that you catch like a firefly, and just like fireflies, you have to release them, because the whole point is that they're tiny and little and need to be with other fireflies. They aren't a pet. They aren't yours to keep. They're just moments. They're just fireflies.

CHAPTER THIRTY-FOUR

Geoff takes me grocery shopping.

It's supposed to be a quick little trip, but it turns into an epic voyage. We don't buy six bananas; we buy twelve. We don't buy five apples; we buy twenty. We buy healthy stuff. No more Cocoa Krispies.

We take it all out to Geoff's car and I'm eating a peach in the front seat and it's dripping everywhere and, you see, this is the problem with fruit. It only *seems* portable and convenient. Turns out you need a hazmat suit and six towels to eat a peach. Guess what that's not true for: Pop-Tarts, Cheetos, I could go on. . . .

"Oh, crap," Geoff goes. "Here comes Dwight."

I lean forward and look out the window, and even though we don't go to school with anyone named Dwight, I fall for it, and then the smell hits me.

"Jesus Christ, Geoff," I say, and I lift my T-shirt and cover my nose. "Seriously, you should see a doctor."

He rolls down the window and starts laughing so hard, the Corolla swerves. My stomach does too.

"Seriously," I say, "you should be ashamed."

I let an appropriate amount of time go by before dropping my collar, but, Jesus, Dwight is still here, like an uncle at Thanksgiving whose stories last *wayyyyy* too long and never have a punch line.

"Seriously," I say again. But then I start laughing because the other choice is vomiting, and my stomach is having too good a time with the ice cream cake to say goodbye to it already.

We pull into my rocky driveway. I'm thinking maybe we should whip up some lemonade for old times' sake, but I let the thought go. We unload all the groceries super quietly, because Mom is asleep in the sunroom, and then I walk G. back out to the car and I take a paper towel to wipe up some of the peach juice on the seat, and I swear to you Dwight is still lingering in there like a nightmare fog and it makes us laugh again.

We make some vague plans for Geoff to come back in a couple of hours with some "tools" to finally put in the new AC, and we're still laughing about That Lingering Dwight!—but before I let Geoff go, I stop laughing, and I pull my old phone out of my bookbag, and I hold it up for him to see.

Geoff looks at it weird, like it's an ancient Mesopotamian tool.

"I thought—I don't know," I say. "I thought we could turn it back on together." Deep breath. "Geoff, I have to tell you something." Deep exhale. "Annabeth died right after sending *me* one last tex—"

"Win, I know. Everybody knows." He puts his hand on my shoulder. "Literally *everybody* knows. It was on the news."

Ignore. Can't compute. I power the phone on and my stomach does every single ride at Kennywood at once. The old cell takes forever to come awake, and in a flash I think that perhaps I'll be saved from reading the message from beyond—Geoff even goes, "Dude, maybe it won't even, like, *register* old texts, since you have a new phone now," when—*ding*.

There's exactly three hundred unread messages. But only one that matters.

I can't look at it. I can't look at it.

I hold it up for Geoff to see. He touches the screen, and then his eyes go watery, but he is somehow made out of smiles.

"**YOU'RE DEAD TO ME**," I texted my sister—after not finishing the college recommendation letter for her teacher to sign; after almost two decades of not appreciating the *A* to my *Q*—and right before she ran the red light without her seat belt on, she wrote—

"Read it, dude," Geoff says.

I flip the phone around.

"**grow up, win**," it says.

CHAPTER THIRTY-FIVE

After Geoff drives off, I walk two steps at a time upstairs and I keep up the pace till I reach my desk, where I wake up my laptop and decide it's time to finally do it. To finish the damn screenplay.

And here's the thing: I don't plan out the last fifteen pages or refer to Ricky Devlin's outline or worry about satisfying mythical story beats. I just . . . type. Forty minutes later—that's all a first stab at it took, forty minutes; or maybe six months and forty minutes, depending on your math—I hit print, and pace an infinity loop in my floor until the hot stack of paper piles up, which I grab to take downstairs.

When I wake up Mom, I am crying and so she is too, immediately.

"What is it?"

"Mom, I'm gay," I say, which I didn't expect to say, but there you have it.

She holds my gaze. "I know. I've known."

"Are you—are you, like, disappointed?"

Her face fuzzes over like mine does when I write dialogue, or so my sister used to tell me. "Only in myself," Mom says. "That you'd think you could ever disappoint me." Her eyes well back up for round two. "I just want you to be *happy*, baby." She looks like my sister, who cried at everything. "But maybe you aren't a baby anymo—"

"Did you know about Geoff and Annabeth?"

"Of course, yes." Her voice changes gears. It grinds in the shift. "It was killing me for you not to know. I don't like secrets."

I take a pillowcase off her pillow. We don't have throw pillows; we have full on *pillow*-pillows in the sunroom, to make up for how uncomfortable wicker furniture is.

I walk the pillowcase to the mantel, and I throw it on top of the urn. I can't look at it anymore. It isn't good enough for Annabeth. It's fake.

"Well, that just makes it look like a ghost," Mom says, and she isn't wrong. It looks as if the urn is dressed up in a cheap ghost costume, that amazing Halloween sequence in *E.T.*

"Yeah," I go. "But don't you always kind of feel like she's with us? Like, doesn't she feel like a ghost already?"

"I believe in heaven," Mom says.

"Doesn't it feel like she's always over your shoulder, though?"

"Every minute," Mama says. "Every second."

Now she practically laughs almost, her sobbing is so hard, like a hyena or a volcano. She laughs and I do too, because this is almost joyful, this realization that we get to share something again. Misery loves company and that's not a bad thing, folks. Misery fucking *needs* company.

"I saw fruit in the fridge," Mom says curiously, as a middle schooler might if his parent had laid out a book about how bodies change. My parents never did that for me. Maybe that's why I was the last guy in my class to get armpit hair. My body just never knew the rules.

"Yeah," I say, "I thought we'd have some fruit for once. The red ones are called apples and the purple ones are called grapes."

"Alert the authorities," she says, fast, and I tilt my head at her and she winks at me and I solve a riddle: I got my humor from her. I am hers.

"You never gave me my birthday gift, Mama," I say. I wipe my nose across my arm.

"Oh. Oh! It's being delivered this afternoon."

"Wait. What's bein—"

"Your present. I've been saving up. I ordered you a replacement air conditioner. A really good one, too. A sturdy one." She takes a deep breath. "My new goal is to cut up my credit cards and start paying for everything outright."

"Mom," I say, "that is amazing." And it is, but I'm also

thinking: I've got to call Geoff and tell him to just return the one we bought, and so I go, "Let me make a quick call," when Mom goes: "Fine, Winny. But first you have to tell me what's in your hand."

I look down. I'd forgotten about the whole reason I came downstairs.

"I did it," I say. And then I clear my throat and I look over at the urn ghost and I don't flinch this time. "I finished this screenplay thing I've been working on. Or, I mean, that I *haven't* been working on."

This is where my sister would ask me to read it for her. *Read it to me!* she'd say, *No caveats!*

I hold up the new pages and scan the first lines of dialogue. Garbage.

But still: "I was thinking I could, I don't know—"

"Read it to me?" Mom says, like a question that isn't one.

"Yeah. The last couple pages, anyway. I *just* wrote it, so it's probably gonna be rough, so—"

"Don't move," Mom says. "I'm going to need one of the *red* fruits. I'm going to need strength for this."

And so she gets an apple, and she sits back down on the wicker lounger, and she settles in as if I am a movie—no, as if I am her son, who she just wants to be happy—and I clear my throat again and close my eyes, and count backward from ten.

"Exterior: Ordinary suburban house, day," I begin—and I read fast, because I don't want to hear Mom not laugh at jokes that she doesn't realize are supposed to be jokes. That would crush me. When I get to the final, clunky pieces of dialogue in the screenplay, where my little protagonist, Double Digits, comes home from battle and discovers that everything is different—that his heroes are just ordinary mortals, and that his life has turned out both more heartbreaking and more astonishing than anything a movie could ever attempt to pull off—I am so overcome with grief that Annabeth isn't here, to tell me how to make it better, that I can't keep going. I actually drop the final page of the screenplay, and my head, too, but then I hear Mom crunching and crunching on that apple. Nothing stops the Roberts family from eating.

And when I look up to smile at that, at my beautiful mom crunching away, I also see, out of the corner of my eye, the pillowcase fall from the urn. It lands quietly on the floor. I leave it there and I pick up the last page, and I finish what I started.

CHAPTER THIRTY-SIX

INT. QUINN'S BEDROOM - NIGHT

It's late. Quinn gets into bed and covers
himself head to toe in a thick blanket.

He switches off his bedside lamp. He takes out
his earplugs. And then we hear what he hears
-- the pleasant drone of his brand-new air
conditioner, humming from the window.

The air conditioner is still wrapped in a big
red ribbon, like a car in a TV commercial.

Quinn props himself up, takes off his fake

glasses, and drops them into the wastebasket
beside his bed.

Then he lies back down and closes his eyes.

And he smiles.

FADE TO BLACK.

Acknowledgments

The Great American Whatever began its life five years ago as a sprawling manuscript intended for a grown-up audience. That unpublished book was called "Quinn, Victorious," and featured many of the same characters as the book in your hands— except they were all a decade older, as the book was set ten years after the accident that changed Quinn's life and ended his sister's.

Lots of people aided me in getting *The Great American Whatever* published, whether by reading hilariously long drafts of "Quinn, Victorious," or later—in the case of Cheri Steinkellner, my close confidante and closest prodder—by encouraging me to revisit the book altogether, from page one.

Thank you, then, to the many folks—including the librarians and educators and booksellers and fellow authors who have supported my work since *Better Nate Than Ever* first debuted—who helped get Quinn out of my bedside drawer and onto bookshelves, especially: Andy Federle; Annie Batz; Betsy Morgan; Brenda Bowen; Brooks Ashmanskas; Christian Trimmer; Christin Landis; Eliot Schrefer; Jason Snow; Karen Katz; Kevin Cahoon; Krista Vossen; Marci Boniferro; Matt Roeser; my parents, Lynne and Mike; Rick Elice; Rob Thomas; Tom Schumacher; Wendi Gu; my *many* vivid bullies within the Upper St. Clair school district; and the all-star staff at Simon & Schuster—particularly my editor, David Gale, and his assistant, Liz Kossnar.

Special thanks to Ellie Batz. This isn't her story, per se, but I could never have told it without her.

Lastly, thank you, *you*, for making it this far. And if you feel like you have a story you have to tell, tell it.